Witchy Woman

&

Other Tales

Tell-Tale Publishing's 7th Annual Horror Anthology

Tell-Tale Publishing's 7th Annual Horror Anthology

Witchy Woman & Other Tales

Tell-Tale Publishing Group

Swartz Creek, MI 48434

Printed in the United States of America

Ric Wasley

Rob Tucker

Darren Simon

Shawn D. Brink

Francesca Quarto

Elizabeth Alsobrooks

TABLE OF CONTENTS

Witchy Woman

Ric Wasley

"Com-on, pick up!"

Brian Sullivan, or Sully, as every male in his clan had been tagged since the first Mick from County Claire had stumbled ashore in the unwelcoming port of old Yankee Boston over a hundred and fifty years ago, muttered into his aging Apple iPhone.

He sighed and wondered for the millionth time why he was still bustin' his pick against the granite ribbed heart of Riona Sinéad O'Cleirigh.

Sully remembered the first time he'd met the black-haired, green-eyed Irish beauty… though to be fair while beauty like hers was a rare event at Callahan's, Irish girls were not.

In fact, anyone not of Irish descent, or at the very least born and raised within the three square miles that comprised the historic Irish enclave of South Boston, 'Southie' to the locals, would have stood out like the proverbial sore thumb.

Not being Irish enough for Callahans was definitely not a problem for Ms. O'Cleirigh - though being referred to by the more modern version of the original surname was.

He'd once introduced her as Riona O'Cleary and she'd icily corrected him. Noting that, "O' Cleirigh is the earliest known of the famous Irish clan names because it was written that the lord of Aidhne, Tigherneach Ua Cleirigh, died in County Galway back in the year 916 A.D."

"In fact," she had told him, "that historic Irish name may actually be the earliest surname recorded in all of Europe."

And that wasn't the first time he'd been put in his place by Ms. O' Cleirigh, who was able to make him feel like the dumb ass hanging on the corner he'd been before he'd worked himself into the computer science program at Northeastern University.

The old crew from the neighborhood still gave him a raft of shit about how he'd become the "Goodwill Hunting" character from the Matt Damon movie and to be fair, they weren't far off.

Witchy Woman

The difference was that, unlike that movie, he intended to trade up his Southie roots for a top-floor condo in the Seaport District or one of those classy red brick Federal front places on Comm. Ave or Beacon Hill.

The last ring on Riona's phone tripped the answer response and her cool modulated voice asked him to leave a message.

Unlike most of the girls he'd been with, her message didn't end with the usual perky promise that she'd get back to him ASAP. And he knew from frustrating experience that she probably wouldn't. But it did end with the soft farewell of, "Go líontar do lá le draíocht". Which after a few quick passes through Google Translate he'd figured out meant, "May your day be filled with magic."

Leaving a Gaelic message on her phone was weird enough but suggesting that anyone in Southie might be interested in having a 'Magical Day', was more than optimistic.

The message finished and he hung up without leaving one.

There wasn't any point. She'd see he'd called and would know what he wanted without any message.

He wanted to see her again.

And no amount of asking or even pleading was going to change that.

She either would or wouldn't and she'd decide in her own time and in her own way.

Maybe she'd call, or just happen to be at a bar or restaurant he dropped by, or perhaps even show up at his door - with no call or explanation. Just a cool smile and a quick but electrifying kiss that would start the banked fires of desire burning for her all over again.

Those times were the best and the worst.

And they always came just when he thought he'd finally suffered through the cold turkey of wanting her so bad he felt like taking a long walk off Fan Pier but was finally getting over her and then… without warning - there she was.

And he was hooked again.

She had that power over him - and he was sure that he wasn't the first or even the only one.

She didn't come on or even flirt. No tight clothes, Tramp Stamp tats, or even heavy eye makeup like most Southie girls. But then again, her eyes didn't need it. They were dark and deep with an indefinable hue that shifted up from emerald green to dark green to sometimes as jet black as her raven hair.

Same with her lips. A dark ochre crimson that glowed with warmth and tantalized with temptation. And yet he'd never even seen her apply the tiniest touch of lip gloss to them. Not even after his best efforts that should have left any commercial lipstick smeared all over his face. Those lips remained as cool and as tantalizing as though they had never been sullied by the touch of any mortal man.

That was part of her mystique. She gave bits and pieces of herself - but never the whole thing. And never enough. Never.

Loving her was like a drug.

You knew it was bad. Hell, you even knew it would eventually kill you.

All your friends told you that you had to quit. Taper off - cut back. And if that didn't work, then cold turkey.

They'd even tried interventions. Fixing him up with cute girls from Southie, JP… even a BC grad student.

And he'd tried too.

He'd dated, mated, and prevaricated. And he thought that his recovery was coming along nicely.

And then... just when he was sure he'd purged her out of his system and the raw bleeding cut of her absence was gone and just starting to scab over, his cell phone had vibrated like a rattlesnake preparing to strike and he'd read the words in ambient blue text.

"Call me. I need you."

Five words. Five banal, simple words. A hope? A command? A plaintive plea? A desperate cry for help? A restorative request for reconciliation?

Or... the cruel tease of a feline fisherman who allows the gasping prey the hope that it might finally escape back into cool waters only to have the sweet claws sink into its flesh once more.

Caught.

But he wanted to be.

No, he didn't.

He thumbed off the text and headed off to Callahans and the latest attempt of his 'Southie Bros' to fix him up with yet another Band-Aid for his bleeding heart.

Witchy Woman

And when he met their latest substitute for her he was pleasantly surprised by her easy laugh, short dirty blond hair, hazel eyes, and a light dusting of freckles on a pleasant face resting nicely atop a trim athletic body that workout clothes hinted might be worth breaking a sweat over.

When the crew drifted away through the necessity of early morning work or classes the next day, he sensed she might have said yes to a drink at his place, And yet...

And yet, there was the nagging warmth of the cell phone in his pocket with the unanswered text.

"Call me. I need you."

So instead of doing the smart thing and inviting the pleasant girl home for a drink he politely excused himself and made the call he always knew he'd be making.

It rang.

And then it rang again.

And on, and on, and on. Until just before he was going to press the red button to terminate a low voice whispered, "I knew you'd call."

He wanted to tell her, "Fuck you!" Or... "Get lost bitch." Or any one of a hundred things

"

he'd thought of when she'd dropped out of his life without warning or reason.

But instead, all he could say was, "Yes."

He could sense her slow smile at the other end of any one of a thousand cell towers and millions of digital pathways.

He waited for her to say, "I've missed you."

Or… "I'm so sorry I had to leave - here's what happened."

But he knew she wouldn't. And in this he was right.

"Do you know where Prides Crossing is?" she asked without preamble.

"It's up near Marblehead and Gloucester - right?"

"Can you be up here by midnight?"

He should have told her, "Are you fuckin ' nuts?" And hung up.

Instead, he looked at his watch and said, "Yeah - but I've got a few questions of my own. Like …"

"I'm texting you the address."

Then she broke the connection.

***

Witchy Woman

The ride up to Prides Crossing was mostly by the heavily traveled old Rt. 128 now Route 95 corridor but the normal commuter traffic being absent he made the trip in about an hour.

The address proved more problematic.

Everything was fine until he got off the highway and started following a meandering country lane through an overhanging layer of oaks and poplar. He glanced at the map and it told him to turn left onto Winding Tree Lane - and that was the last clear reading he got.

Soon his GPS stared that irritating little multicolored dot spinning and it wouldn't clear up.

He thumbed on his phone and tapped on the map but got the same irritating spinning followed by a frozen screen. He wasn't sure if he should be amused or alarmed that the blue dot of his car showed up in the middle of the blank screen as though he'd fallen off the edge of the world.

A sign?

A warning?

Or just one of those dead spots between cell tower handoffs?

Finally, he mentally shrugged his shoulders and continued following the aptly named Winding Tree Road until it eventually petered out giving him a choice of a wooded archaic dirt country road or a stone bridge over a small stream surrounded by sullen-looking bog.

He chose the bridge.

She had said, "I'll be waiting at the end of the road - don't let me down."

"Don t let me down."

'What an arrogant bitch', he thought.

And then just as quickly told himself, 'Right - and yet here you are still dancing to her tune.'

His hands gripped the steering wheel tighter.

What was it about her that made him drop everything every time she called?

Was it her or him?

Was he just a pussy-whipped asshole, a fool for a woman who had invaded his soul?

Or was there something more?

Was it love or lust or a combination of both?

No, it was something more.

Witchy Woman

Something that went beyond logic and hid in those dark corners where rationality wilted in the face of indefinable longing and perhaps even a bit of overly romanticized superstition.

But of course, while he suspected he had inherited more than a bit of the romantic Irish poet in his heritage, he didn't believe in superstition - did he?

The bridge led to a single-track dirt road that seemed to get even narrower as the trees closed in around his car.

Soon he could hear the scraping and squeaking of small branches and bushes running their leafy fingers over his paint job.

Great, he grumbled mentally. *So much for those two hours spent waxing it last weekend. The things we do for love.*

He smiled but it all but died on his lips when he turned a corner, slipped between two oversized rhododendron's and came to a dead end.

Just like that. The road stopped. Right smack in the literal middle of nowhere.

The was just a small clearing in the trees and a few overgrown bushes that looked as though they might have been ornamental at some time in the distant past.

He put the car in park, turned off the engine, and got out.

Nothing. Silence.

No breeze, no sound.

The thought that he was in the middle of all this nature without even insect noise crawled up his spine.

He checked his phone's GPS. Still nothing. Only now even his little blue dot of digital self-awareness was gone - like he'd ceased to exist.

OK, that's it.

He thumbed to his contact list and tapped her number.

More silence.

He glanced at the upper right-hand corner of his iPhone and confirmed what he should have known. No bars. No signal. A true Dead Zone.

Why was he not surprised?

Fuck it.

He opened the door and climbed back in but as he hit the ignition button he called out to the silent words, "Hey - I tried!"

Suddenly his phone vibrated in his hand.

He looked at the screen.

Witchy Woman

"Take the path between the two stone Wyverns and follow it to the house. The front door is open."

"What is a Wyvern and where are they?" He typed back into messenger.

He hit send but nothing happened except a few seconds later the green-lit scroll appeared beneath it telling him 'message not delivered.'

Of course.

He looked up at the bars - still no signal.

But how had she gotten through?

He slid the phone back into his pocket and got out of the car again.

OK. Time to go Wyvern hunting… whatever the fuck they were.

It took him almost fifteen minutes but as he was making his second and more careful circuit of the clearing, he noticed what appeared to be a stone claw peeking out from under what at one time must have been some large arboreta bush.

He pushed back a large feathery frond and saw a six or seven-foot cement statue of a dragon hidden by the overgrown bush.

At first, he couldn't see a path or even another stone statue but going by the text he kicked the matted leaves on either side until he uncovered another clawed foot about a dozen away from the first.

That meant that the path had to be in between, so he put his head down, held his forearms against his face pushed between a pair of large branches, and presto - just like that he slid through and found himself on a white gravel driveway that wound between hedges and more ornamental shrubs.

But these didn't look overgrown. They looked well-tended and cared for. Almost as if the bushes obscuring the driveway were there to exclude cars, people, and perhaps the entire 21st century.

He walked up the drive, the gravel crunching under his feet and as he rounded the curve of the box hedge, he saw a small pillared portico set in an ivy-covered red brick federal style 18th-century country house.

The door was open.

He walked in.

The pale blue interior smelled of old wood, beeswax, some sort of spice incense, and the must of accumulated centuries.

And something else.

Witchy Woman

Something strange, yet familiar that hovered just beyond his recognition.

He glanced around the foyer.

Polished cherrywood decorative tables displayed silver ornaments and blue glass figurines.

The walls were dotted with 18th-century portraits and pictures of ships and landscapes and a large brass chandelier suspended from the ceiling.

Beyond that… silence.

"Riona?" he called.

A hand brushed his neck from behind.

He jumped and turned.

"Jesus! You scared the piss outta 'me!"

She smiled. "Welcome to my home."

***

"Tea or whiskey?" she smiled as they sat in the strangely eclectic room that must have been the parlor back when federal-style country houses entertained their guests in an intimate setting.

The molding and scroll work was still evident in the classic federalist colonial decor in the foyer and front rooms and it appeared that this one had been eclectically updated to something between a 1930's Berlin Bauhouse style and a 1960s Haight Ashbury funk.

After scaring the crap out of him with her sudden appearance from nowhere she'd cheerfully ignored all of his questions by snuggling into his arms and wriggling artfully against him - all the while leading him into the parlor crash-pad where she installed him on a pile of overstuffed cushions that looked like they had been transported straight out of 1001 Arabian Nights.

And if that weren't enough to complete the surreal illusion the 3-foot-high object in front of them was nothing less than a Moroccan water-style hash pipe that looked like it belonged to Jimi Hendricks or on the Cover of the Beatles Sargent Pepper album.

She raised her head from his shoulder, a small enigmatic smile playing about the corners of her mouth.

"Or… if you're not thirsty," she gestured to the brass and glass water pipe, "I have many interesting mixes that are guaranteed to,'take your mind for a ride."

He snorted. "You know I had a couple of Vietnam-era uncles and I'm well versed in

60's and 70's music. So, I know you're copping a line from an old Boston song, 'Com'on let us give your mind a ride'."

Her eyebrows turned up. "So…?"

"So, that's decades before your time."

"Really?"

"Hell, it's decades before mine and I'm older than you."

"Don't be so sure."

"What…?"

He looked down at her, but she was already pushing herself up and away.

She put one foot under her and rose gracefully to a standing position, and stretching like a cat, said softly, "So what will it be - coffee, tea or me?"

He laughed. "And I know you got that from somewhere else too but it also seems to be long before my time. Remind me again what you're studying at BU and MIT and Harvard and all the other places you're monitoring classes. Is it Pop culture or Anthropology?"

She paused at the sideboard crowded with a hodgepodge of oddities of a hundred cultures from India to China and said, "Neither."

She returned to the cushions with one delicate white hand around a bottle of Bushmills Irish Whiskey and a lump of dark tarry substance.

He pointed to it. "What's that?"

She grinned and winked.

"The stuff that dreams are made of."

"Ha! I know that one!" He reached out and drew her back toward him.

"You my girl are in the presence of a Turner Classic Movies aficionado and I never miss a screening of Bogey, Mary Astor, and Sidney Greenstreet in the Maltese Falcon."

"My, my…" She batted her long eyelashes at him theatrically. "I am in the presence of a true film buff."

"The feeling is mutual."

She poured him two fingers of the Irish whiskey and watched while he drained the heavy crystal glass with a quick tilt of his head.

She leaned forward and gave his whiskey-wet lips a slow swipe of her tongue that turned into a lingering kiss.

When it finally broke, he pulled away and took a deep breath.

Witchy Woman

"Ok, while I still have the slightest chance of thinking straight I do have to ask you one cogent question."

She said nothing, only continuing to observe from her green/gold eyes.

"Why the fuck am I here?

"Does there have to be a reason?"

"Well, from your call I assumed so."

"Maybe I was just lonely."

"That need could be fulfilled by any man who saw you."

"Ah, but I don't want just 'any man'. I want you"

She ran her fingers down his cheek and jumped back with a start.

"Damn!" He rubbed his cheek where she'd touched it. "What did you have in your hand?"

She opened her eyes innocently wide and letting her right hand fall open answered, "just my fingers."

He regarded them for a moment and then took her fingers between his palm and thumb and rubbed them across his cheek. Nothing.

He shook his head.

"I d't know what it was but it was like sparks going off against my skin. I could even see the glow crackling from your fingertips."

She smiled. "Probably just static electricity."

He rubbed his arm on the warm damask cloth of the couch and then toughed her bare arm.

Nothing.

"Yeah? Well, if so, it only flows one way."

"Maybe it's just my electrifying personality." She smiled.

"Care to try again or do you find my behavior too, shockin'."

"Rather than more bad puns how 'bout we try this instead."

He pulled her into his lap and began an enthusiastic exploration of her soft body.

He quickly noticed that while as usual she was dressed modestly, though eerily provocative in flowing layers of silk and satin and other diaphanous material - she was also not wearing underwear.

Much later when he finally came up for air and was able to observe his surroundings, he saw that a fire had been lit.

Funny, he thought. I don't recall either of us moving from this spot so who lit the fire?

He also noticed two glasses of a blood-red wine and a crystal decanter. And who poured those?

As if reading his mind she reached over to the small brass-topped table and handed him one of the glasses, taking the other for herself.

As she settled back into his arms he asked, "Do you have roommates?"

She took a long sip before raising her eyes to his and replying mischievously. "Why, am I not enough, or are you just into threesomes?"

He laughed. "No - you're more than enough." He took a sip of the wine. It was heavy and rich with flavors of berries and nuts and smoke and… something else. Something familiar but out of place - in wine.

He must have been frowning because she lapped at her wine like a cat and then swiped her wine-wet tongue across his lips.

"Well then forget about wine and fires and show me."

And he did.

The next time he came back to reality he felt so pleasantly drained that if a tuxedoed baboon had bent over to refill his glass it would probably not have produced more than a yawn.

Then he noticed that the lights were on.

Then he noticed that they weren't.

Oh, the lamps glowing around the room gave off light all right but it wasn't from electricity. They appeared to be old-fashioned oil or kerosene.

He moved a lock of silky black hair from her face.

"Does this place have electricity?"

"Yes... Sometimes. But not for lighting."

"Why?"

"Because I don't like it."

"Kinda hard to live in the modern world without it."

"Who said I liked living in the modern world?"

He gently pulled her shoulder so that she was facing him.

"So you're one of the back-to-nature 'Green 'crowd? No modern devices or science?"

"No, use them where appropriate and I actually have a doctorate in physics and another in molecular biology."

"Whoa!" He sat up.

"So how does that squared with living in the past?"

"I like the past. There was much wisdom there that so-called modern science has forgotten."

"So what do you do then? What's your occupation? Where do you work?"

She stared at the fire. "I work here - For me."

"But doing what? What's your job?"

"I am a bridge between the past, the present, and the future."

"Wow," he chuckled, "that's some responsibility."

"Yes," she said. "It is."

But she wasn't smiling.

Minutes ticked by. From somewhere he heard the low chime of a clock striking the hour. He couldn't be sure, but it sounded like it might have been ten or eleven or even twelve. He glanced at his watch. It had stopped. At ten past twelve. The time that he'd arrived.

He pulled out his phone. It was dead.

He squeezed her shoulder. "Hey. I was gonna phone for pizza but my phone's outta juice. Is your cell working?"

"No," she replied, not looking up. "I don't have one."

"What? Then how did you call me?"

Instead of answering she smiled up at him and asked, "Are you hungry?"

"Ah, yeah."

"Com'on then." She pulled him up from the couch and steered him into a walnut-paneled dining room where a small buffet had been laid out on Wedgewood china and silver-covered dishes.

He hadn't realized how hungry he was and helped himself to some kind of rich game-based stew and fruit and cheese.

Then it struck him.

"So wait a minute? Where did this all come from? You didn't go get it so there's got to be someone else here."

"Not really. I laid it all out before you got here."

He tasted the stew.

"No way. This is hot and it's been hours since I got here."

"Has it? Perhaps time is not what you think it is." She nibbled on some cheese and bit into a grape.

Witchy Woman

"Well, I know that it only runs in one direction and that a chunk of it has flowed by since I got here."

"Has it?"

"OK, I get it. And yes, it does fly when you're having fun. And don't get me wrong, we've been having a whole lot of it, but still…"

She took a sip of her wine and leaned against the long table.

"Suppose your construct of time was based solely because you had so little of it?"

He shrugged. "Well, hopefully, I'm gonna get as much of it as anyone else."

"And how much is that?"

"I dunno. I hope at least eighty or ninety years. There are even folks living to a hundred now."

"One hundred years." She shook her head sadly.

"Do you realize how little that is? How little time to think and explore and create?"

Her languid detachment fell away and she spoke with passion.

"The universe is billions of years old, animal life on earth hundreds of millions of years old, thinking humanoids hundreds of thousands of years, cities and writing perhaps ten thousand years." She paused. She seemed to be staring not at him but at something far away.

"And yet we poor humans have but a few decades to try to understand, create and move forward."

She bit her lip and suddenly her eyes burned as they bore into his.

"Imagine if it didn't have to be that way. Imagine if instead of your eighty, or ninety or even one hundred years, you had hundreds, or thousands or tens of thousands of years to explore and learn and teach and improve… what couldn't you accomplish?"

Alarmed by her intensity he took a step backward.

"I'm not quite sure I know what you're talking about?"

She drained her glass and set it down on the table.

Her eyes had taken on a hard cast that turned them greenish gold and then to steel grey.

"I'm talking about what if you could enhance your brain to use not just the pathetic 60-70% that it does now but 80 or 90 or even 100% of its capacity and neurons."

She grabbed his hand and squeezed until he was forced to squeeze back to keep his knuckles from cracking.

"What if you could unleash the power to bend both time and space? Take the power that the superstitious and ignorant used to believe were reserved for only God or Satan?"

He stared at her for a long moment and then suddenly yanked his hand away.

"What the fuck are you talking about?"

Her pale skin had faded to porcelain white and twin red spots of rage glowed on each cheek.

Then as quickly as it had come - it was gone.

She came around the table and buried her head against his chest.

"I'm sorry. It... it's just this project I'm working on that's making me crazy."

She took his hand and pulled him away from that table, leading him down a long hallway until she came to a closed door.

He pulled back on her hand.

"Hang on a sec, I still got some questions."

She smiled up impishly at him.

"Betcha I know how to make you forget 'em."

She opened the door to her bedroom.

***

Sully was awakened by the sunlight streaming through his window.

But it wasn't a window from some weird stuck-back-in-time house on the North Shore but his own crap pad in Southie.

He swung his feet from the mattress and onto the dirty floor. How had he gotten back home? He didn't remember.

In fact, the last thing he remembered was Rhiona pulling him into her bedroom after which everything became a jumble of tangled limbs, passionate kisses, and multiple organisms… which was great. But how did he get home?

Fuck! Had she called an Uber? Did he have a 25-mile ride back to collect his car?

He pulled up the blinds and look down at the street.

No, the car was in its usual spot.

He was relieved but still puzzled so he called the number he had for her. It rang once and disconnected. So he texted back on her original message to him and pressed 'send'. It came back, of course, 'Message not delivered.'

***

And so it went for the next two weeks until he began to wonder if he had just imagined the whole damn thing.

Get over her and move on, he told himself.

And just when he thought he had, the damn phone buzzed in his pocket.

Sully, please - I need you.

***

This time when he arrived it seemed that the trees and bushes knew him and were not only parted but seemed to welcome him, swaying inward to show him the driveway all the way up to the house. She was standing at the door when he arrived.

She was beautiful as always but there were lines of worry around her mouth and an almost hardness in her eyes.

She kissed him, took his hand, and led him inside.

"Sully," she said without preamble, "I need you to do something for me."

"Well, yeah - I'm fine - and how the fuck are you?"

She bowed her head. "I deserve that. But..." She drew her eyes back to his. "I think I've shown you how I feel about you - right?"

She paused a moment and then leaned up and kissed him.

He tried not to respond but finally sighed and said, "Yeah. So what do you need?"

"Do you still have those drug connections in Southie?"

***

Sully was one of those Southie kids who in every generation decided that getting high, getting in fights, petty crime, and knocking some girl up were not the path to the life he wanted.

But it wasn't always that way.

In high school, he'd run with a typical neighborhood crew and he hadn't been above moving the occasional product for a quick infusion of cash.

Witchy Woman

But that had ceased when he saw a few of his buddies go down for dumb shit that sent them to MCI Walpole for 2-5.

They told him it was bullshit time that they could handle but he decided he couldn't and that a crappy apartment was better than a 6x8 in Walpole.

So, he'd gotten out of the distribution chain.

And now here was this ethereal girl in her North Shore Hobbit hole asking him to dip his toes back into very murky waters.

She had sensed his reluctance and guided him back into the quaint old house and fireplace parlor for a presumable round two of last night's bedroom Olympics. But this time he wanted some answers before she started messing with his perspectives.

So when she pulled him down to the couch, instead of moving toward her inviting carnelian lips, he leaned back against the opposite armrest and asked the pertinent question.

"Why?"

"Why what?" She smiled.

"I was gonna say don't be cute but I kinda like it when you are, so let me be more specific. Don't be disingenuous - you know what I mean by why."

She bit her lower lip.

"Yes. I do. Sorry. After so many years of prevaricating sometimes it's difficult to be forthcoming."

He snorted. "Well, it can't be that many years and if you trust me enough to get you drugs you can at least trust me enough to tell me, why.

I didn't take you for a junkie. Unless… what? The occasional bump of coke?"

She cocked her head, thought for a moment, and then shook it.

"No, I used to use it in certain compounds but I always processed and extracted it from the leaves themselves."

She stared at a point behind him and murmured almost to herself, "After all, back then no one outside of New Orleans or Memphis was offering the powdered variety."

"What are you talking about? Coke has been available on every street corner for the last 50 years."

She looked up.

"Oh, sorry. Of course. Don't mind me. Just wool-gathering."

Witchy Woman

She turned and took his hand.

"But I really need your help, Sully. I need some hard-to-get drugs and I don't know where to turn."

"And I told you I don't deal that shit anymore."

She didn't say anything - just looked at him.

Finally, he sighed.

"I'm not promising anything but what exactly is it that you're trying to score?"

She brightened, then gave him a serious look.

Some of it will be easy - cocaine, heroin… Even the psychedelics shouldn't be too hard, peyote, LSD, and the rest of the psychotropics. But there is one that has eluded me for decades."

"Decades?" He interrupted incredulously, but she seemed not to hear him.

"It had a name when I used it last but I'm sure it's probably called by something else now."

She took his hand in both of hers.

"And that's why I need you, Sully. I wouldn't even know where to begin looking."

He pulled back.

"You still haven't told me anything about this drug. Let's start with what was it called and why kind of high did it give?"

She shook her head.

"It wasn't a drug like that. It wasn't a sop like gin or laudanum or now heroine - to give the hapless, helpless, and hopeless an alternative to their bleak existence."

Her lip curled in contempt and then her expression softened. "Though God knows I've seen enough over the years to understand that for many, numbness might be the best they could hope for from their sad lives."

She bit her lip and then seemed to shake the feeling off.

"No, this drug… no, let's say, 'compound', has the opposite effect.

It doesn't dull the senses, it enhances them. You might even say expands them."

Her eyes became distant. Her voice grew softer. "It crystallizes clarity - enhances perception - expands the receptors of every cell in your…"

She broke off suddenly and refocused her eyes on him. Almost as if she had said too much.

Witchy Woman

The flirting smile returned to her face like a mummer's mask at a Renaissance ball - all happy and fun-loving. But now he knew, she was hiding something.

It must have shown on his face because she gave him a sheepish grin and said in a broad comic brogue, "Sorry, it must be the Irish in me talkin'," then added mischievously, "But I supposed to a Sullivan Boy-o you can find it in your heart to forgive a poor Irish lass from waxing poetic, can't ya now?" She giggled, leaned forward, and kissed him.

"And so maybe I can make it up to you?"

And she did.

***

Later, just before he fell into a satisfied sleep she whispered, "You won't forget now…"

Only half awake he mumbled, "No, no - I'll check tomorrow. I got a guy I know - Tommy Doughty, who can probably hook me up with whatever you need."

He pulled her closer until her cheek rested on his chest, then closed his eyes and yawned. Then opened them again. And said sleepily, "Oh - yeah… I guess you should tell me what the fuck is this drug/compound or whatever the fuck it is, called?"

She didn't raise her head but very distinctly said, "Back in Ireland it was called, 'Eagan'."

"That's a strange name."

"It's Gaelic."

"What does it mean?"

She turned her head slightly so that her chin rested on his chest, so for a moment, he could see his own eyes reflected back in her glittering green/gold ones as she whispered…"Wisdom."

***

And that's how he found himself back at Callahan's meeting up with Tommy Doughty in a back booth in the corner near the kitchen.

"What the fuck bull-shit name is that?" Tommy said as slammed back his second shot Bushmills - on Sully's tab. But he supposed he shouldn't care Riona had said money was no object when it came to getting what she needed.

Witchy Woman

"She said it's Gaelic. For Christ's sake Tommy, don't give me that, your Granny spoke it all the time when we were kids."

"Yeah, yeah," he muttered. "But never understood what the fuck she was sayin'." He took another pull at his long-neck bottle of Pabst and sighed. "I may know a guy who knows a guy. But it's gonna cost."

"Just get it and then we'll talk price."

***

Weeks went by and he didn't hear from Tommy or Riona. And as much as he longed to be with her he was starting to think that maybe Riona, her mysterious drug, and the whole thing was better left to simply letting the whole affair slide into the oblivion of aborted relationships, his phone rang.

"Sully?"

"Yeah?"

"It's Tommy."

"Yeah?

"I think I may have what you want."

***

They met back in the same back booth in Callahans and Tommy opened by saying, "Who the fuck is this stuff for?"

"Yeah - And how the fuck are you, Tommy?"

"Hey man, no disrespect. But you know I gotta lot of deep connections and most of 'em never heard of this shit."

"And so if it's a problem why did you call me?"

Tommy's little weasel eyes darted around the noisy bar, then he cocked his head.

"I didn't say it was a problem. I got a line on it from a connection in Belfast but it's gonna cost you."

"So you said. How much?"

"Fifty… Large."

"Fifty?! Are you smokin' your own shit?"

Tommy spread his hands. "Hey man, I don't make it and I don't set the price. I'm just the middleman. Sure I make a few bucks, that's how I live. But I gotta tell you I had to run down some serious shit and wade in deep before I found anyone who even heard of it and even then they weren't all that anxious to do business."

"Why? Drugs are drugs. Why do they care?"

Tommy slammed back another shot and blinked several times

"Look, the only thing I know is that they said they had to get it from an old lady in Cork who is batshit crazy."

"Yeah, and so?"

"Well, she deals in plants and herbs and all kinds of hallucinogenic shit. You know, like peyote and magic mushrooms but Irish style."

Sully took a sip of his Bushmills but said nothing.

"Anyhow, the way I get it is that a few years ago some kid from Dublin ordered some stuff from her but tried to stiff her on the payment."

"And?"

"And they found him three days later in a Dublin alley. He had gouged out his own eyes and chewed off all of his fingers."

Sully drained the rest of his Bushmills.

"Well, that sucks for him. But you can get this stuff?"

Tommy nodded. "Yup. And that's why it's gonna cost you fifty large - and no questions asked."

Ric Wasley

As Sully got up from the booth and started for the door he heard from behind him…

"And no refunds."

***

That's what he'd told Riona… funny how her cell always worked fine when he was calling her about matters important to her…

But two hours later he got a text telling him to check his bank balance and found it was up by $75,000.

"Seventy-five grand?" he asked when she picked up. "The price is Fifty."

"Sure," she said then added in a comic Irish lilt, "And can't I be givin' me, darlin' boy, a wee present then?"

"A twenty-five thousand dollar present? What for?"

He could sense her smile through his iPhone. "For makin' me toes curl Darlin'."

"Jesus - I'd do that for free."

***

And that was why he found himself turning off the paved road onto the winding track that lead to the weird old house that didn't seem to want to be found.

As usual, the GPS wasn't working and as usual, he came to a complete stop in the middle of the woodland clearing without a hint of where the ever-elusive driveway would choose to appear.

This time he didn't get out but simply powered down his window and called out, "Hey! Magic gate or trees or whatever the fuck you are, I'm here and if you don't open up I'm gonna turn this heap around and go back to Southie and Ms. Riona is gonna have to whistle for her very expensive shit!"

Nothing happened.

He waited.

One minute passed.

Then Two.

Then Three.

When his phone showed him five full minutes, he put the car in reverse and muttered, "Fuck this!" He pushed the car into a reverse spin then shifted back to drive and … stopped.

Because there, right in front of him was the driveway. Beautifully manicured. Gates wide open and the house lights glowing in the distance.

For one brief moment he thought about taking his foot off the brake and continuing back out to Rt. 95 and saying bye-bye, to hidden driveways, haunted woods, and spooky old houses forever.

Then he thought about the soft pale skin and mesmerizing eyes of the girl waiting at the end of that driveway.

He sighed, turned the wheel, and drove through the gates.

***

This time she was waiting at the door.

She kissed him then took his arm and led him through the house into the same paneled and fired place room they'd enjoyed so thoroughly before.

An open bottle of wine was sitting on the sideboard, and she stepped back to let him pour.

He picked it up to do so but stopped when he looked at the label. CHÂTEAU LATOUR A POMEROL 1929.

Witchy Woman

He didn't know all that much about fine wines but he did know that anything that was pushing a hundred years old had to be pricey.

"Riona?"

"Yes?"

"Where did you get this bottle?"

She didn't look up.

"Which one is it?"

"The CHÂTEAU LATOUR A POMEROL."

He deliberately neglected to tell her the year.

"Oh, it was probably when I toured the winery. We all bought a case of that year's vintage. That's probably the last bottle. I simply must go back someday and pick up another case.

He took the two glasses back and set the bottle down with the label facing away from them.

He poured and they clinked glasses before taking a sip. It was amazing.

He said so and she smiled.

"Glad you like it."

"And you say you bought it from the vineyard you toured in France?"

"Uh, huh."

She took another sip.

"And when was that?"

"Oh, I dunno, a few years ago."

"And it was that year's vintage?"

"Yes… hey, what's with all the questions? You writing a book?" She laughed.

"No." He held up the bottle.

"Not unless it's a history book 'cause this vintage was bottled nearly a hundred years ago."

Her eyes narrowed but she said nothing.

He continued, "So how could you have bought a hundred-year-old vintage unless you're pushing something like a hundred and twenty years old!"

"You're wrong," she said.

"It's not a hundred and twenty… it's closer to two hundred and twenty."

***

His first reaction had been to laugh. The second was to say, "Fuck you. How dumb do you think I am?"

But the look on her face told him that she really believed it.

Witchy Woman

So his final reaction was to get the hell out of there because cute and smart though she was, she was also full-on batshit crazy.

But he didn't do any.

Wasn't it Shakespeare who said 'Love makes suckers of all?'

Probably not, but he should have.

In the end, she held on to his hand and said, "Let me tell you a story."

He wasn't sure what it would be but he was sure of one thing. It wouldn't be boring.

She continued.

"In 1817, in Donegal, a little girl was born to a woman on the fringes of society. Her husband had gone to America to seek his fortune and had found work as a pick and shovel man on the Erie canal.

She wrote him of their new daughter, and he promised he'd send back passage money for her and the child but it never came nor any other word from him ever again.

So like millions of women from time immemorial she raised her daughter as best she could and made her way by selling herbal remedies, potions, and salves for man and beast, along with delivering children, livestock, and mending broken bones."

She paused and took a long sip from her wine glass.

"And as mothers do, she taught her daughter those healing arts and some older arts as well."

"What older arts?" he asked as he poured another for himself.

She stared at the yellowed, peeling label on the bottle.

"Those that have been passed down since the Druids fled England for Erin in the time of the Romans."

Her eyes glowed in the firelight.

"You see they had divined that the relationship between man and nature and the universe was but a thin veil that separated what was, to what could be."

His brain was reeling. Was it the wine or her words?

He poured another glass but put it down.

He shook his head.

"What are you saying?"

She looked up at him, her strange shifting colored eyes boring into his.

"I'm saying that the ancient wisdom of the druids had opened the doors to the power of unleashing not just the tiny fraction of our minds we use now, but to the possibility of more - much more. And how to unlock it - all of it"

He put his glass down and looked at her for a long moment. Then asked softly, "And you've found how to do that?"

A small smile played across her lips. She stood up and took his hand. "Come…" was all she said.

***

"What hell is this?"

He looked around at the rough granite walls that made up part of the original stone foundation of the old house.

It was a strange combination of low ceiling, dark corners, and thick, stained plank tables covered with beakers and test tubes, juxtaposed with state-of-the-art modern lab equipment.

She tugged on his hand and led him to one of the tables where a large electron microscope had been set up.

She took a glass slide from a tray and then pricked her finger with a needle from a sterile packet. She let a drop of blood fall onto the slide and placed it under the microscope.

She stood back and motioned him forward. "Look."

He peered through the lens and saw the wiggling cellular motion but it was nothing he didn't expect.

"So?"

She held out her hand.

"Now give me what you got from your friend."

He paused for a moment and then reached into the inside pocket of his leather jacket and pulled out a sealed packet of bright red crystals.

He eyed the small packet. "Yeah, and at fifty grand this has gotta be worth more than diamonds."

She took it. "It is."

With tweezers she plucked a single crystal no bigger than a grain of salt, dropped it into a test tube of solution, shook it, and then put a drop onto the slide.

"Now look."

He did.

Suddenly the blood droplet was going crazy. Expanding, dividing, forming new patterns until it was almost unrecognizable.

"What the fuck? What's happening?"

Witchy Woman

"The same thing that will happen to the billions of neurons in a human brain when this compound is introduced into the bloodstream.

Expansion and enhancement of every cell in your body - But especially your brain."

He stared at her without speaking, trying to process what she was saying.

Finally, he shook his head. "What exactly do you mean by enhancement?"

She switched off the microscope and walked over to a whiteboard on the wall.

"How much of your brain do you think you use on any given day?"

"Is this a rank or some kind of a joke?" He smiled, thinking of his buddies down at Callahan's.

Almost as if she had read his mind she grinned, "No - at least not in your case."

He grinned back and then shrugged.

"I dunno, about half?" he said and then thought for a moment. "Wait. I think I heard someplace that it was actually only about 10%. Is that right?"

She picked up a marker and wrote 50% on the whiteboard, then next to it, 10%, with a big question mark between them.

"Do you know how much it really is?"

"Apparently not," he shrugged.

She turned back to the whiteboard and wrote 100% and underlined it with a flourish.

"Really? So where did the 10% thing come from?"

It was her turn to shrug.

"Urban myth, self-help gurus, and a lot of misunderstood science. Researchers who have studied the brain with magnetic resonance imaging technology have found that there are no dormant parts of the brain. In fact, most of your brain is active almost all of the time."

She drew an arrow up to the 10% and circled it.

"Many scientists think that it got confused with the percent of neurons that make up your brain cells. Care to guess what that number is?"

Sully pointed his finger like a cocked pistol at the whiteboard and said, "Boom - 10%"

She grinned and gave him the gesture back,

"Bingo."

"Now," she said, becoming serious again, "What if you could enable that other 90% of your brain cells to have direct and conscious access to that 10% of neurons?"

"I dunno. What could you do?"

She turned to him, eyes blazing. "What couldn't you do!"

She crossed back over to him and took his hands.

"Imagine if instead of being mere pathways for electrical/chemical receptors you manipulate and direct each neuron and cell consciously."

He shook his head. "How could you do that?"

She pulled him closer. "With another chemical/electrical enhancing compound."

"Does anything like that exist?"

"Yes."

"Where?"

"Here." She opened her hand and showed him the package he'd brought her tonight.

"And this stuff makes it happen?"

She nodded, then took out three small baggies filled with white powder and laid them alongside the first.

He squinted at the trio of thumb-sized packets then pulled back and looked at her. "Are those what I think they are?"

She nodded. "Cocaine, heroin. and crystal meth."

He shook his head bewildered. "Damn! I never pegged you for a crackhead."

She laughed.

"I'm not. This stuff is merely a tool. A spark to kickstart the engine if you will."

"You see, I've had access to the compound, though in very small amounts, many times over the years. But it always took too long to activate and of too short a duration to achieve what I was looking for."

"And what exactly were you looking for? And what does it do?"

She took a step back and leaned against the workbench.

"Let me answer your question with another question. How old do you think I am?"

He laughed. "Oh no you don't. I'm not that dumb."

She smiled back. "Don't worry I grant you complete dispensation and promise to continue to bone you no matter how wrong you are."

He laughed again. "Deal. Ok, then, early to mid-twenties. Although if you really bought that wine when you said you did, you must be pretty well preserved. But physically, yeah certainly, early to mid-twenties."

She smiled wolfishly. "Suppose I was to tell you that I am nearly ten times older than that?"

"So then what you're saying is that you really did pick up that wine a hundred years ago?"

"Yes, and that was just to replace the case I'd gotten one hundred years before that one!"

***

There were a lot of things that he wanted to say but he rejected each one as soon as he thought of them.

The first time she said her age he'd figured that she was goofing on him or simply delusional.

But now he found himself wondering, was she delusional? Or was he for not admitting to himself that everything about the unsettling but oddly alluring woman before him was anything but normal?

She inhabited a strange world of roads that led nowhere. Driveways that appeared and disappeared. Tables that set themselves and wine that found its own way to your glass.

And above a woman who puzzled and beguiled and perhaps even frightened him a bit. Yeah… but delusion seemed to have taken a back seat to the drabness of the world when he was not around her.

So… He drew in a deep breath and then slowly let it out in something between a sigh and a growl.

"Let's say I buy your story - and I'm not saying I do - but just how is that possible?"

She was serious again.

"That's where this comes in."

She held up the baggie she'd laid out fifty grand for.

She continued, "As I told you, when I was a girl in Ireland my mother was a herbalist and a healer, like her mother and her mother before her going back to ancient Celts and beyond back to the peoples of pre-history that the old ones called the Fairie Folk.

They had cataloged herbs and mushrooms and leaves and mosses - dried and brewed and boiled poultices and potions for thousands of years. And eventually, by accident or design, they had learned what alone and in combination, they could use to heal the mind and body."

Her eyes looked past him at something only she could see.

"And one day ages ago one such herbalist/healer/wise woman, combined certain rare leaves and compounds and found that strangely enough, they gave her the power to command the functions of her own body."

She moved closer and grabbed his hand.

"She and her fellow practitioners found that not only could they instruct their body to shake off disease but repair itself from small wounds and minor accidents.

Over time they learned how to direct this repairing process to the very cells in their bodies to not only heal themselves but to actually slow the aging process itself. They refined and perfected the process until they could extend the life of the average woman who would have normally been old by thirty and dead by forty, to fifty, seventy-five, or even one hundred years of age. And by the time the 'knowledge 'came down to me... to over two hundred years old."

He wasn't sure he was buying it but he asked. "So you're saying that you're immortal? That means Ireland must be crawling with all these old ladies who look like teenagers!"

She shook her head. "No."

"Why not?"

"First because their numbers were always very few. But mostly because they were still human. The products of their time, their upbringing. The culture and values they were raised with. Most who extended their lives wound up falling into despair at the loss of husbands and children, family friends, and the world they knew and understood. And after a century or even two of life, they simply stopped taking the compound, and death soon followed."

"But why didn't they just give their husbands and children the magic dust so they could all live together, happily ever after?" He winked.

He expected her to laugh but she didn't. She just looked sad.

"As the 'Immortal Bard 'said, 'Aye, there's the rub'. You see the compound doesn't work on men - only women." She shook her head.

Witchy Woman

"It has something to do with the Y chromosome. I'm still studying it. Maybe someday…" Her voice trailed off. She drew a deep breath. "And that's why most grew to weariness and despair watching their sons and husband grow old and die."

He put both hands on her shoulders and set her at arm's length.

"But you didn't. You kept with it and you're two hundred. Why?"

She stared straight back at him and then drew herself up.

"Because I have erased superstition with science," she said fiercely.

"I understand what this can truly be. No disease, no illness - no death." She clenched her fists. "And if I can solve these last problems, then maybe for everyone!"

His head was spinning. But at the same time, he was fascinated. If this was true… no illness? No death?

He swallowed and asked a question. The question. "Could you… could you do this for me? Could you make it work on a guy?"

"Yes!" She answered without hesitation, and then stopped and seemed to consider for a moment. "At least I think I could. If I can optimize the crystals," she paused, "I think I could find a way around the Y chromosome."

She drew another deep breath. "I'm so close." She bit her bottom lip and sat down again. "Just a few more experiments and with the new compound and an increased dosage of this…" She pointed to the packets of heroin, coke, meth and the blood-red crystals laid carelessly on the workbench.

"So you really intend to combine your magic dust with these killers?" He asked warily pointing to the drug packets.

She shrugged. "If that's what it takes - yes."

He squeezed his eyes shut and rubbed them with his thumb and forefinger.

"Jesus, Riona, that stuff will make your brains run out of your ears."

She nodded her head. "When taken by themself, yes. But when used with the compound and the other stimulants I believe it will open the receptors on the other cells just enough to let me create billions of new neurons and thus achieve complete control of every cell in my body."

Her eyes were sparkling again.

Witchy Woman

He knew he was beaten. Either she was totally nuts or about to pull off the greatest feat since mankind swung down out of trees.

He didn't know which and was quite frankly too tired and confused to even think about it.

He doubted she even heard him when he said, "Be careful."

Finally, he simply said, "See you later." And quietly closed the big front door.

***

He tried, unsuccessfully, not to think about her over the next few weeks and had almost succeeded when his cell rang again and she said without preamble, "How soon can you get here?"

"Well, hello to you too. And how have you been?"

"Don't waste time," she snapped, "you need to come right now. I've got something to show you, something that you will not believe."

"I dunno about that…" he managed to say before he realized he was talking to an empty line.

When he got there the covering bushes were gone, the gate was wide open and the driveway clear all the way up to the house.

He pulled up and got out and then spun around just catching a sparking glimpse of something before it vanished into the bushes.

Not knowing what else to do he walked up to the door and was surprised to have it opened by a… butler?

"Good evening, sir," he said in a plummy British accent. "Please step this way."

He followed, wondering when she had gotten a butler and more puzzling … why?

The butler ushered him into the old-fashioned parlor and then bowing said solemnly, "Madam will be with you shortly," and left.

He sat there bemused for a few minutes, listening to the ship's clock on the mantel tick until without warning the polished wood double doors swung back and a vision of light clad in silver and gold drifted in as if on a cloud.

Beams of light radiated from her and around her almost blinding him.

The vision drifted over to him and smiled serenely.

Witchy Woman

"Greetings mortal. And what favor have you come to beg of the elf queen?"

"What?" He tried to shade his eyes with his hand. "What the fuck - elf queen?"

She gave a tinkling laugh. "What, mortal - you never saw Lord of the Rings? Don't you recognize Queen Galadriel of the Elves?"

Holy shit! Yes. That's who hovered in front of him. It was that character from the Peter Jackson movie. The freakin' elf queen! He'd only tried LSD once long ago but maybe he was having a flashback.

It must have shown on his face because the elf queen giggled and said, "Oh I'm sorry, Sully. That was mean of me but I just couldn't resist it."

As she spoke her skin began to ripple and her features changed in a few moments and Galadriel become Rhiona.

His mouth must have stayed open while she threw herself into his arms and bubbled, "I did it!"

"Did what?" he asked shaking his head.

The giggle died on her lips, replaced by fierce pride.

"Complete success! I now have conscious control over every cell in my body."

He drew in a deep breath and let it out again. He felt like he had fallen down the rabbit hole along with Alice but he had to ask, "So is that what I just saw… the Elf Queen?"

She positively beamed.

"Yes!"

"And the butler who ushered me in…?"

She bowed in an elaborate curtsey. "That was me too!"

He knew he shouldn't be surprised but he had to ask… "So you did it? You can change, control your appearance?"

"Not only that but physically alter every cell in my body.

I can literally will myself into any shape, size, or configuration I can imagine."

Her eyes took on a strange glaze.

"Watch!"

Her skin rippled again, then began to bubble and flow like warm putty. It expanded, grew taller, darker, and developed claws and scales until it morphed into a… dragon! A full-fledged Disney/Hobbit-style dragon. Would it breathe fire?

As if it had read his mind the dragon winked and blew a fiery smoke ring.

Witchy Woman

Moments later it was Riona once more who flopped down on the couch next to him giggling uncontrollably.

She laughed until she hiccupped a few times, then wiped her eyes and grinned, "Convinced?"

He rolled his eyes and sighed. "How could I not be?"

She snuggled into his side and wiggled her toes. "I've done it, Sully. Everything that kings and priests and witches and wizards have sought since the dawn of time - and I've done it. Complete control and immortality."

She put a finger to the side of her cheek and then amended, "No not just immortality - omnipotence."

"Oh, come on."

"No really." She spun around and took his hand. "Give me any test. Any shape, age, or form that living cells can take and I can achieve it." Her eyes took on a mischievous glint."Name your favorite animal, storybook character, historical figure…" she leaned in, kissed him, and breathed, "your sexiest woman fantasy."

"I'm fine with things just like they are…"

She jumped up and brought her laptop back to the couch.

"Who's your all-time favorite sexy female rock star?"

"Stevie Nicks," he replied without thinking.

She typed in a few words on Google and a YouTube MTV video of Stevie came on. "Just watch."

Sure enough, in less than a minute a perfect facsimile of the famous rock star was smiling next to him.

"Convinced?" the faux Stevie smiled up at him.

The eyelashes fluttered and the lips puckered, and he bent to kiss her before he noticed the eyes behind the eyes. He pulled back and the image fluttered - quicker now as she seemed to be gaining experience - and he found himself again beside Riona.

He noticed that she was looking somewhat pale and even drained.

She closed her eyes and leaned back against him and yawned.

"Oh, sorry." She stretched. "This is all pretty new and I need to concentrate more of my control on the recovery process." She leaned up and kissed him. "But never fear, I'll learn…" She yawned again, closed her eyes, and snuggled back into his chest.

"I'll learn," she murmured and fell asleep.

***

Weeks went by, then months. He tried to call but there was no response. No voice mail to leave a message. Same with text - they bounced back as 'not delivered'.

Then, just when he had almost succeeded in convincing himself that it had all been some kind of a drug-induced fever dream his aging iPhone rang, and without even looking, he knew. It was her.

"Sully." Her voice was strange. It was her but not her.

He knew that she could change into anyone or anything she could imagine but he sensed that something beyond that was not right. Her voice seemed to modulate, change pitch, and timber. A little girl, an old lady, a cartoon character, a man, a woman, and even something with a growl that sounded like a lion.

So when she begged with a quavering voice that was for just a moment, her own - and said only, "please come." He did.

***

The driveway was overgrown and the gate was rusted shut but he got a tire iron out of the trunk and forced it open.

The previously luxuriant plantings had browned and wilted as though struck with blight and the front door looked weathered and warped in the doorjamb.

He pushed it open with his shoulder and it screeched and scraped as though it hadn't been opened in years.

Inside the air was close and musty. And silent.

"Riona?" he called. The house swallowed his voice.

He worked his way back into the interior, calling.

There was no response until…

He heard sobbing coming from down a dimly remembered long corridor. He followed it until he came to what he remembered as her bedroom where she had taken him that first night.

Witchy Woman

He found her there on the bed, curled into a fetal ball, eyes red and wet, hands clutching and unclenching.

She didn't seem to see him until he came and sat down next to her. He put his hand on her shoulder. "What happened.?"

At first, she seemed not to recognize him, then finally looked up at him with terrified eyes… "I can't control it."

***

"What do you mean?" he asked and put his hand on her shoulder to raise her up. But a moment later he had his answer.

Her features rippled and in an instant changed into those of a teenage girl with blond hair and innocent blue eyes. He blinked and shook his head. "Tiffany," he whispered because he was staring down at his first high school girlfriend.

"Who?" the image asked.

Realizing it was Riona he muttered, "my old girlfriend from high school. But how did you know her?"

"From you."

"That's ridiculous. I haven't thought of her in years."

"It doesn't matter. She's still in your memory and when you touched me I was immediately in touch with every cell in your brain."

"But why her in particular? We only dated in high school and it was no big deal. Why would your enhanced power pick out her?"

The image had changed back to Riona and there were tears on her cheeks.

"I don't know." She swallowed and whispered, "Because I can't control it."

***

They sat at the kitchen table drinking some sort of herbal tea as she tried to explain what had been happening in the months since he had seen her.

"At first it was fantastic," she said with a sad smile. "I experimented with every sort of configuration that individual cells could take. Not just people but animals too. I could take the shape of a dog or a cat..." she grinned. "Hell, one night after a few glasses of Pinot

Witchy Woman

Grigio I even became a dragon and flew out over Marblehead harbor!"

The grin quickly faded.

"But then I began to notice something odd." She bit the inside of her lip. "When I woke up in the morning I felt different."

"Why?"

"Because I was."

"What did you feel like?"

"No, you've got it wrong. I didn't just feel different, I was different. Physically."

"When I looked in the mirror I would see a different person." She paused, then shuddered, "Or thing."

"Why?"

"At first I couldn't figure it out. - then I realized that although I was asleep, my brain wasn't."

She sat up straighter. "As we know, our brain never sleeps. Every moment our lizard brain is operating with basic life responses and functions. And then of course there are dreams… " She swallowed. "And nightmares."

She hugged herself and shivered.

"Have you ever had a terrible nightmare and been so relieved when you woke and realized it was just a dream?"

"Sure. Who hasn't?"

"Well, suppose when you woke you found that the dream had followed you home?"

"Meaning?"

"Meaning that the people and images from your unconscious mind were now physically manifesting themselves on your conscious mind, and your body was transforming into them without your conscious thought."

She grabbed both of his hands in a desperate grip. "Sully, I can't control it."

"But I thought you said you could consciously control all of your cells. Has that changed?"

She shook her head. "No, I still can do that. But I can't keep it in conscious check every moment of every day. And if I stop, whatever is rolling around my subconscious mind automatically manifests itself on my body."

She began sobbing in earnest. "Do you know what it's like to have to focus continually to keep yourself from changing - your conscious mind battling with your subconscious?"

Witchy Woman

"Sully," she raised her tear-stained face to his. "I think I'm going insane."

***

He held her and the minutes ticked by in even, tonal clicks from the big ship's clock.

When she finally was breathing quietly against his chest he said, "What can I do to help?"

She was quiet for a moment, then rose.

"There is only one other thing I can think of."

"What?"

She smiled for the first time and said in a heavy brogue, "Oh, me Boyo you've heard of the, hair of the dog?"

"You can't possibly mean…"

But she just turned and walked straight for the cellar door that led down to the laboratory.

He followed her shaking his head.

When he got down she was already mixing the compound in an old stone mortar and pestle.

Well, he thought, at this point, she might as well go all the way with full witchy woman.

He came up behind her and said, "Don't you need a caldron and perhaps a broom on standby?"

"Very funny," she muttered and kept on crushing the crystals to a fine powder.

He noticed that she was adding more and of the compound than she had on the previous occasion.

"Hey, take it easy with that stuff. Besides, I thought you said you were already maxed out at 100%?"

"I am." She didn't stop working. "At least I thought I was."

She stopped and turned to look at him.

"But maybe," she said as if she was trying to convince herself as well as him, "there is still some small portion, a tiny crevice of my subconscious brain, that remains beyond my control. That is what I hope one final massive dose will be able to break through to finally give me total mastery and stop the subconscious transformations."

She stopped pounding, then poured the powder into a small beaker filled with a blue liquid which she heated over a Bunsen burner.

Witchy Woman

It quickly boiled and she placed it on the bench to cool.

While it was cooling she open a drawer and took out a sealed cellophane package which she ripped open revealing a syringe and a length of flexible tubing.

"Oh come on." Sully reached over to take her arm but she swatted him away.

"No!" She shook her head fiercely. "This is the only way."

"You'll kill yourself!" He reached for her again but the arm he grabbed swelled in size, grew red scales and fingers that sported three-inch claws. Her eyes glowed a fiery red.

"Remember, I can become anything I want."

"Yes," he said quietly. "And a lot that you don't."

The arm returned to her original proportions and she nodded, saying softly, "I know. That's why you have to let me try."

He finally nodded and stepped back.

She filled the syringe with the blue liquid, then wrapped her arm to find a vein and with a quick push of the plunger, injected herself.

He wasn't sure what he expected but it certainly wasn't what he got.

At first, he was afraid that she died because she gave a gasp and stood straight up on her toes - her legs and arms outstretched as if she was being electrocuted. Her skin rippled and her eyes flashed through dozens of different colors. Her hair flowed and curled around her face in every hue and style imaginable.

He didn't know what to do. All he could do was stand and stare, Until…

Her skin began to glow with a golden radiance as if she was lit with a bright candle from within.

The glow continued to grow and so did she until the brilliance was so bright that he had to hold his hands up to block the blinding light.

There was a high-pitched keening accompanied by a wailing undulation that make him want to curl into a ball and wrap his arms around his head.

Just when he thought he could not take it another second, it stopped.

He lowered his hands and suddenly the golden radiance exploded into thousands of tiny particles of light that floated and darted around the room like mad fireflies.

Witchy Woman

One minute they drifted by like golden snowflakes, then tiny pixies, and then micro cosmoses complete with suns and planets.

They swirled and danced around him, warming him, caressing him, murmuring in his ear. "I've done it, I've done it, I've done it…"

The golden cloud was all around him, in every part of his body, in every pore of his skin. He could feel her within him. Gliding through his mind, his bloodstream, the air in his lungs.

He was standing in the doorway to the house and he could feel her leaving him, coalescing into the golden light.

"Wait - don't go!"

He could feel her slipping away.

"I must. I'm changed. I'm no longer Riona. I have become… something else."

She was gone from him now and it was like a drug withdrawal - a physical ache.

The golden light was fading back into the house, dimming and dispersing.

"Will I ever see you again?" he asked hoarsely.

"Yesssss…" floated back the answer.

"When?"

"Whenever you think of me and sometimes…" there was a tiny laugh, "when you least expect it."

***

He didn't remember leaving or even the ride home but a week later he went back to the house and he couldn't find it.

The clearing was overgrown with saplings and the driveway had vanished. But he kept looking and finally he was able to uncover the paw of one of the lion statues and squeeze himself through the rusted gate.

The door to the crumbling old house tilted drunkenly on its hinges and when he entered the entire structure looked as if it had been abandoned for centuries.

The fine furnishing and antiques were gone. The settee they'd shared before the fireplace was no more than a pile of rotted wood and moldy fabric. Every room was covered in a thick coating of dust.

He started back toward the front door and then on impulse turned toward the bedroom.

Witchy Woman

There was something on the rotted old bed right in the center. Something bright and shining.

He picked it up and turned it over in his hands. It was a pendant. A golden pentagram on a chain with a sparkling emerald in the center.

Emerald. For the white witch from the Emerald Isle.

He slipped it over his head and left.

***

Over time he tried to forget about her and there were times when he thought he'd succeeded.

Then for some reason, he'd see someone catch his eye.

A man, a woman, a boy, a girl, young or old, wise or whimsical. They would nod at him and smile - sometimes even grin and wink.

In fact, sometimes he would have sworn that it was a dog or a cat or a bird or a squirrel that cocked its head and looked at him impishly.

He had eventually met a girl, fallen in love and gotten married, and had a beautiful little daughter with emerald green eyes.

And he had forgotten all about the magical, mystical Riona… Almost.

Many years later when he had finally relegated the entire thing to a strange and wonderful memory deep back in the musty closet of his mind, his doorbell rang.

It was Halloween eve and he was carving a pumpkin for his daughter.

He was up to his elbows in pumpkin seeds so he called to her. "Sweetheart, can you get the door? It's probably some early Trick-or-Treaters."

"OK, Daddy," she called back.

Then she called breathlessly… "Daddy, come here!"

He grabbed a dishtowel and wiping his hands walked into the hallway.

She was on her knees holding a jet-black cat.

"Look Daddy, this must be a magic cat 'cause she rang the doorbell."

He smiled and knelt down, picking up the cat.

Witchy Woman

Mostly for his daughter, he said with a smile, "Well, kitty, is that true? Are you a magic cat?"

The cat stretched out and nuzzled against his cheek. And then he heard from - he could never figure out from where..."You bet your ass I am, me Boyo. Happy Halloween!"

The cat licked his face like a quick darting kiss, then leaped from his arms and vanished into the darkness. And from somewhere far away came a bright, tinkling laugh.

The End

Selfie

Rob Tucker

As an investigative journalist, I was secretly able to interview one of the victims isolated in her home, as long as her name and image were withheld.

I came across the social problem when my sister told me what had happened to a friend of hers. I was a few years older than she was and beginning a career in television journalism.

It suddenly occurred to her friend that her selfie photo was smirking at her. Her expression was not beautiful and alluring like she intended. Almost daily, she tried different tops that exposed her cleavage and tight shorts that accentuated her narrow waist and curvaceous long legs.

At first, she blamed the cell phone. She thought maybe there was something wrong with it. She took photos of herself because it was fun and gave her something to do. Otherwise, she was bored. The photos created a permanent visual record, not like staring critically at herself in the mirror where her image vanished when she moved away.

Influenced by photos of attractive young women and fashion models in the media, she thought that with a little cosmetic application and styling and shaping her luxurious hair, she could look just like them. Anyone who saw her on social media would think she was beautiful and special and admire her as a personality. She might even be discovered.

She practiced flirting expressions with her wide brown eyes and thin dark brows. Pursing her lips with a slight upturn at the corners and striking provocative poses conveyed how womanly she was.

From what I could gather, stealing her identity was child's play for D. Hacking was for amateurs. Why bother with hoarding the personal information of young women who posted selfies when he could steal their physical and spiritual essence and add them to his growing collection.

Discovering and identifying targets was easy enough. Once he had digitally lured and abducted them with the promise of being the mystery man in their lives, he toyed with their insecurities he now possessed.

He appealed to their need to display and advertise their modified physical appearance. He recognized the signs of being feminine enough and wanting a relationship with a man. He sent them phrases of endearment and how much he admired how they looked and that he couldn't wait to meet them.

Being preyed upon sent a universal spasm of fear through the victims whose lives were entombed in their cell phones. Friends could no longer text and email or even call each other. They struggled with themselves to leave their houses. They lost their appetite for food and pleasure of any kind. Every effort made to crash against their enclosure encountered an elastic bubble that would not burst. They were trapped.

They wanted to know who D was but couldn't access their phones or computers to attempt to trace D. They existed in a purgatory from which they could not return. No one could help them. They stopped changing. They stopped growing. They were frozen in time.

ROB TUCKER

BREAKING NEWS
(On Camera)

Social media has taken a turn for the worst. The recent discovery of depression and mental health issues in young women is now attributed to the hypnotic effect of cell phone addiction. Most noted is the time spent taking and digitally sharing selfies.

Psychologists are seeing more and more female patients demonstrating symptoms of identity dysfunction and self-deprecation.

Social media sources have denied responsibility for the phenomenon, stating that they have no influence or control over cell phone use behavior. They won't even acknowledge the existence of D because they can't figure out who D is. In addition, they argue first amendment rights must be taken into consideration.

Religious parents and friends believe that an evil demonic source is behind the epidemic, and it lures victims through subtextual codes that ensnare unsuspecting users.

SELFIED

Technical experts have not been able to identify or trace who or what is behind the scheme, which is now considered by the FBI as a new kind of abduction.

Conspiracy theorists have jumped on the bandwagon that what is happening to selfie addicts is a form of anti-feminism whose purpose is to undermine feminist beliefs and political agendas by neutering and removing them.

Short of recalling cell phones and shutting down all social media, efforts to block unknown hidden messages are not successful. Experts and authorities recommending the recall of cell phones or at least the removal of the camera software function have been met with a wall of resistance.

According to a poll, most selfie addicts are calling the movement against them a hoax and are willing to risk abduction, LOL.

If you or anyone you know has information that could lead to the identification of D, please contact the FBI at your locally listed phone number. Your identity will not be shared or revealed. Anyone who is an insider and is willing to come forward as a whistle blower will not be identified and will receive personal witness protection by the FBI.

You are encouraged to not be intimidated or extorted by D, whoever or whatever he is.

End of Message

Even though I had to read those lines from a teleprompter in a television studio, I wasn't satisfied. Young women were being exploited by D whoever or whatever. I couldn't just report on the aftermath and psychological suffering and carnage D was causing. I had to do something more. Even though I hated and despised social media, the only option left to me was to become a selfie addict and allow myself to be abducted into D's damaging sordid world.

That's what I did and that's where I am now. So how am I able to write this?

Suffice to say I am not a happy camper. Trying to take down D is well outside my expertise and job description. But when you're a journalist, you do whatever you have to do to get the story.

I still don't know who D is and I can't escape from being imprisoned in my selfie.

SELFIED

The only thing I have to work with is that my selfie is no longer the real me. I can be a trickster too. My selfie is not who I am.

I'm an attractive (requirement of the job), highly educated, well-adjusted journalist, married to a loving husband and raising two awesome children. I appear on nightly television as a staff journalist. I'm a role model for young women aspiring to career success.

My challenge is to activate my alternate selfie persona as a spy infiltrating the world of D and releasing all the young selfie women he or it is holding captive. I maintain a psychic connection to my selfie slave. D is not aware that my communication has not been severed as he has done with the other selfie-napped victims. Still, my selfie spy has a monumental task of decoding and negotiating the labyrinthine enigma to find, outsmart, and take out D, what some call an impossible task and a dangerous journey into an alternate reality from which I may never return.

The Dead vs. The Dead

Darren Simon

I dropped to my knees, my chest heaving, lungs burning. My hand, coated in gore, shook uncontrollably. Brains and skull fragments clung to the blade I grasped. The revolver in my other hand stunk of spent gunpowder. All around me the twisted human bodies of the Undeads I'd just wiped out lay crumbled in heaps, like trash covered by swarming flies.

Sweat dripped from my dampened, thinning hair. Down my forehead. Into my eyes. They stung, forcing me to blink rapidly. Or maybe I blinked in disbelief as to just how fucked up this damned supply run had become.

There were ten of these undead bastards, each in a different level of decay. Some had transitioned some time ago. Their skin, covered in maggots, peeled back from their bones, revealing their rotting insides. Others had changed more recently, their flesh a bloody, torn mess. Entrails hung loosely. Gray lifeless eyes were buried deep within their skulls.

All stunk of rancid meat and vinegar.

Two children, probably no more than eight or nine when they'd transitioned, were among the corpses. I couldn't take my eyes off them. They looked so peaceful now, like porcelain dolls, after I knifed them through their heads. Just a heartbeat ago, they had hissed and squealed and tore at me like wild beasts.

They reminded me of my own kids. I lowered my head to my chest. Hot tears filled my eyes. Ben and Isabel had been so young. How could I have failed them? Why couldn't I keep them safe? Because I had been weak then. I let our home be invaded while I wasn't there. I let those monsters ravage my kids and my wife. Why had I left them unprotected? I heard their screams as I reached our house, but I was too damn late. The house was overrun. Their cries of agony were burned into my brain. It was an endless ringing in my ears that got worse during my dreams.

I should have charged and joined my family in death, but I was a coward.

THE DEAD Vs THE DEAD

Damn me. I didn't even have the courage to give them peace. Instead, I watched them transition and march off with the rest of the Undeads. I condemned my wife and kids to become these mindless, sad beasts feasting on human flesh.

I wiped the tears away, my thin fingers sliding across my bony, rough cheeks. This wasn't like me. I didn't cry anymore. I was little more than a rat scavenging to survive.

I slowly started to control my breathing. My hands shook less. I gazed at the sky, squinting at the sun of a sweltering mid-summer afternoon in the South. My AC/DC T-shirt and faded, ripped jeans were baked to my skin, clinging tightly to my limbs, like heavy wet rags. A hot breeze brushed against my face and rattled the leaves in the trees just beyond the abandoned church I stupidly chose to investigate.

Its stained-glass windows depicting Jesus' ascension were covered in muck and mostly shattered. The cross atop the bell tower was split in half, hanging loosely from a few remaining wooden splinters. A flock of crows sat atop the roof, watching the carnage without a care. Why should they give a shit about the apocalypse? What should nature care if mankind wiped itself out? Probably all the better.

I glanced back at the two children, their eyes forever closed, their bodies finally at rest. One of them still wore a golden Cross around her neck. "I'm so sorry. I wish I could have—"

A shriek erupted from behind me. Before I could react, a beast pounced on my back. Jagged teeth punctured my neck like tiny razors and ripped through my skin. The creature's hot putrid breath, reeking like rotten eggs, engulfed me, seeping through my nose, gagging me. Bloody saliva drooled down my neck onto my shoulder.

I thrashed my arms wildly until my elbow crunched through bone in the beast's face, forcing it off me.

Swinging around, I came face to face with what once was a woman. A bloodied, moldy white dress hung loosely over her emaciated frame, her flesh nothing more than puss-filled sores over patches of rotting skin. Half of her face had either been eaten away or the skin simply slipped off her bones. She probably once had long blond hair but now just strands remained, flowing wildly around her exposed skull.

An inhuman hiss slid from her bloodied lips. Bits of my own flesh hung from her teeth. Her eyes, gray orbs surrounded by a sea of red, stared through me. She titled her head back, sniffing the air with what remained of her nose, her tongue flicking back and forth.

Ignoring the stabbing pain in my neck, I gripped my revolver in one hand, the knife in the other. I studied both, then holstered the gun. The crack of a fired round could bring more of them. Besides, I only had two bullets left. I couldn't waste them. I needed one for me now. *Son of a bitch!* That thought squeezed my brain like a vise slowly twisting tighter and tighter. My temples throbbed. Lifting my knife, I backed away from her, giving her space to launch her attack. "Come and get me. Finish what you started."

As if some part of her understood, she screamed, then leaped at me with surprising agility, but I was faster. I sidestepped, grabbing her neck with my freehand and wrestling her to the ground. My fingers pierced her paper-thin skin, reaching the wet, meaty tendons of her throat. She clawed at me with yellow fingernails. Her teeth snapped, and her spit-filled hiss grew louder.

"Say goodbye, you undead bitch." I plunged my blade into the side of her head. Her skull cracked. The knife dug into her brain. I twisted once, then twice, to make sure a true death came to her. Black goo slid from the gaping hole. She wheezed, a final gaseous breath that stunk of split pea soup left out for days. Her eyes rolled up into her skull, and her body went limp. Lifting the blade away, I stumbled backward away from her, falling to the ground.

Dropping my knife in the green grass, I reached to my neck. My fingers probed along the shredded skin. Taking a deep breath, I then gazed at my hand. *Dammit.* My own blood dripped from my fingertips.

"Fuck me."

My pulse raced and my stomach convulsed. I could taste her putrid breath. Hot bile rose up my throat and poured from my mouth. When it was done, I lowered my head to the wet earth.

"How could I have been so stupid?" I pounded my fist into the ground. "I let one of those bastards get me."

THE DEAD Vs THE DEAD

The bite mark wasn't big, but it burned like fire. Of course, it didn't need to be big. She'd penetrated my flesh. Her saliva was already coursing through my body. I could literally feel it—like acid burning through my veins, scorching my insides.

Death was coming for me. I shook my head, gripping my hair as if to rip it out strand by strand. My mind raced. Maybe the bite wasn't deep enough. Maybe it was just a scratch. Maybe I was immune to the sickness. Bullshit. It was over. I was… over.

I started to laugh uncontrollably, like a chicken's cackle. In a rage, I grabbed my knife, then jumped on the dead woman. I plunged the blade over and over into her face, crushing what remained of her cheek bones and skull until her brains splattered over my hand, up my arm and even splashed against my lips and cheeks.

Still, I laughed wildly… until my mind quieted, until I could think again. I wiped her slimy brain bits from my lips and peered over my shoulder at the dead.

"No damn way am I going to become like them." I cleaned off my blade in the grass, then painfully climbed to my feet. Shallow breaths raced through my mouth. I staggered around, searching for the pack I'd dropped when the herd attacked. "There's got to be a way."

"Come on, where the hell are you?" I didn't want to let go. I didn't want to go out like this. My body shivered. The blood rushed from my head. A sense of emptiness made my gut hurt.

"I said, where are you?" My fists tightened until my knuckles turned white.

Finally, I spotted it next to one of them. "There you are!" My body tensed, and I stumbled toward my old, cracked leather supply pack. Grabbing it, I then lumbered up the church steps, through the heavy wooden doors hanging from their hinges.

My insides ached. It was probably just my imagination, but I could swear I felt the sickness snaking through my body.

But maybe I had a chance, and that's why I crossed into the church.

I needed the tools to spark a fire.

The Undeads had left their mark inside the church hall. How many had died here? How many had transitioned here? Light spilled in through the broken windows, casting shadows across the wooden floor littered by shattered glass and chairs pushed on their sides. Handprints outlined by dried blood covered the walls. Flies spilled in and out, buzzing around me, nipping at my shredded skin. I covered my nose with my hand to block out the stench of death, worse than sour, spoiled milk, but it didn't help. The odor was trapped inside this forgotten place of prayer.

My eyes watered. Maybe I was smelling my own flesh starting to rot.

I spun around, scanning the destruction. I just needed paper I could fasten to a tree branch to build a torch. I had matches in my pack. I'd ignite the torch and use it to sear the wound. Maybe it would burn away the sickness before it seeped into my heart and my brain… just maybe.

There, underneath an overturned chair I found what I needed—a Bible. I felt myself smile and shook my head. "What do you think, God? You've taken a lot from me. Mind if I take one of your books and rip out a page or two? What do you say, Lo—"

A hand grabbed my ankle from behind.

My heart stopped. Insides froze. A deep breath lodged in my throat. I twisted around, whipping out my knife. "Son of a bitch." God had given me an answer.

A priest still wearing his white collar lay at my feet, his body ripped in half, his intestines dragging behind him. His gray lifeless eyes almost hidden behind a blackened, bloated face gazed at me. He chomped his teeth and groaned as if his hunger could never be satisfied.

I kicked my leg free, then knelt to the beast. "Priest, if there's a God, when you see him, tell him to go to hell. Tell him John Taylor said so." The priest ignored my words, his hands reaching out as if to bless me.

"Goodbye." I drove my blade into his skull. He flinched, then lowered his head to the floor. His gray eyes remained open in a forever stare. Placing my boot against his head, I ripped out the blade, then wiped off his bones and brain juice from the blade on his black clergy shirt.

I gazed one more time at the Bible. "Fine, I'll leave it." Peering around, I found a pile of blue paper at the base of a pedestal at the front of the church where the priest would have led Sunday services. Slinging my pack over my shoulder, I inched my way to the pedestal. The blue paper turned out to be a stack of newsletters.

The date at the top was from two years ago. That's when the sickness began… when the *Undeads* began to feast on humanity. "This will do."

Stealing a few sheets, I slid them into my pack, then made my way to the entryway. Peeking through the doors, all seemed quiet outside. No signs of any more beasts. The only movement was from the growing number of flies covering the corpses, feasting on their dead flesh.

"All right, Johnny boy, you know what you have to do." Leaving the church, I scrambled away from the undead horde I'd massacred. I just couldn't be around them anymore. Not far away was a row of cherry blossoms. I longed for their sweet smell, anything to shake the stench of death here. Standing above them were larger oaks, their dark, bent, twisted branches a sad contrast to the vibrant pink of the blossoms. Still, the oaks could provide just what I need to build a torch.

I staggered across the countryside, sweat dripping from the sides of my brow. My legs shook as if they wanted to cave. I tripped and stumbled along the way, nearly falling but somehow, I stayed on my feet. My shoulders hunched. Each breath felt crusty and burned inside my chest. The sickness was already taking me, or maybe I was just exhausted under the oppressive heat. I moved slower and slower, slogging through tall grass, but I had to keep going to save my life.

Once at the blossoms, I paused once to breathe in their gentle fragrance, but nothing could erase the rancid odor of rotting flesh that burned the inside of my nose and lodged in my throat. My heart sank. My body felt so heavy, I wanted to drop to my knees.

"Fuck it." Shaking my head, I reached for an oak branch hanging just over my head and ripped it away. I used my knife to sharpen one end. Then I wadded up copies of the newsletter, jabbing the branch through the paper. *Hurry, fucker.* The bite in my neck had become numb. My head felt light. I wanted to close my eyes and sleep, but if I did, I'd never wake up. I'd become one of them. No, I had to fight for as long as I could. I hadn't lived this long in this ugly reality by just giving up.

Rats are survivors.

THE DEAD Vs THE DEAD

Reaching into my bag, I found the matches. I struck one match, but it didn't ignite the paper. "Come on!" My hand trembled. I struck a second match. Still nothing. My vision blurred. My heart pounded in my ears. My sweaty fingers could barely hold the matches. I struck a third and failed again. *Please! Work!*

The fourth match did the job. My body untensed. My eyes bulged. Yes! A tiny flickering orange flame danced and crackled to life. I let it grow, holding my hand over the fire until it burned my skin.

The time had come to char my wound, the only chance I had to save myself. "Come on, do what you have to."

Taking a deep breath, I inched the flame closer and closer to my neck. Gritting my teeth, closing my eyes, I thrust the fire against my torn flesh. I bit my tongue to hold back a scream. The salty, metallic taste of blood filled my mouth. My stomach roiled as the stench of my own sizzling skin overtook me. *Keep…going.*

Burn…the…death…away. I cried out in silence, then I felt nothing.

Darkness engulfed me.

DARREN SIMON

***

I heard myself cough, a phlegmy mucous rising from my throat. My chest heaved. I coughed more, drops of spit running down the sides of my mouth. My body convulsed, and my eyes fluttered open.

Nighttime had blanketed the tall grass fields of the countryside in a dense, heavy darkness. It was one of those humid, sweaty moonless summer nights with a murkiness so thick you can't see but a few feet in any direction.

Yet I shivered. I guess that meant the sickness hadn't taken me quite yet. I still knew my name— John Taylor. I remembered my kids' names and my wife's beautiful face. I remembered our home, and how much it meant to paint it and fill it with furniture and memories.

But deep inside me something was wrong. Ice seeped through my veins, and my body shook uncontrollably. I placed my fingers against my face. My skin was cold and clammy. My hands and feet were stiff. Stabbing pain shot through my insides, burrowing through my bones and muscle. I cringed to suppress a cry.

There was a void in my gut that made my stomach gurgle, but I had no hunger—not even any thirst.

I reached for the bite mark with shaky hands. I tried tilting my head, but it was as if the fire had fused my flesh. My fingers probed my charred skin. Patches flaked off, falling onto my shirt. I could only imagine what it looked like, but had it worked? Had I saved my—?

The sound of dried leaves cracking under footsteps sounded just a few feet away. Painful groans inched closer.

Shit.

I held my breath and sniffed the air. The familiar stench of rotting, decaying flesh scorched my nose. Still, my body shook, but now more violently.

More leaves cracked behind me. Teeth gnashed. The *Undeads'* hissing surrounded me.

Shit.

I slowly lowered my quivering hands into my pack and reached for a book of matches.

Shit.

I struck one, igniting a tiny flame just bright enough to split the darkness a few feet in front of me.

I gasped. Stomach twisted. A swarm of gray eyes glared at me from all directions through the dancing orange haze. Corpses dragging broken limbs and ripped entrails through the grass slithered toward me.

Shit.

I dropped the match and slid away on my backside until I slammed into a tree trunk. Without the dim light of the match, I could no longer see them, but their groans were like a chorus of death all around me.

I reached for my gun, but the holster was empty. My mouth dropped open. The damn thing must have fallen out, but it had to be close. Find it, fucker. Move. I frantically ran my hands through the grass, but the gun evaded me. I shook my head. Shallow breaths raced between my lips.

My only other weapon was my knife. I dropped my hand down to my belt where the handle of my blade should be, but it was gone, too. No! No! No! The revelation that I had nothing to protect myself felt as if a mule had kicked me in the stomach. I blindly searched through the grass again and came up empty. It was too late anyway.

The hissing was almost on top of me.

I wrapped my arms around my chest. I lowered my head and mashed my back against the tree trunk until jagged ends of the bark cut through my skin.

A skeletal hand gripped my leg, and I kicked it away. "Stay the fuck away from me."

They didn't listen.

More hands grabbed my legs.

"No. God. Please."

The Undeads clawed along my body, dragging their broken and twisted remains from my thighs up to my chest. I squeezed my eyes shut and buried my face in my hands. "I hope you all fucking choke on me."

I waited for them to tear into my flesh, to rip my chest open and feast on my heart. But they didn't. They wrenched my hands away from my face. A tongue slid across my cheek, leaving a trail of putrid saliva along my skin. With my eyelids squeezed tight, I twisted my head away. Another tongue, icy and wet, licked at the other side of my face.

Beasts above and beside me hissed and groaned into my ears, seemingly whispering of their hunger for my skin, my blood, my organs. Their bloody saliva dripped over my head, down my face.

"What are you waiting for?" I screamed.

The beasts only hissed back at me.

I forced my eyes open and stiffened my body. I didn't dare move or breathe. I tried to stop my hands from trembling. Five of them, with skin hanging loosely from their skulls, maggots crawling around their mouths, sniffed me like a pack of ravenous dogs. Their heads wobbled back and forth as if their necks could barely support them. They took turns rubbing their pulpy, blackened faces against my neck, licking my wound.

I bit my lips to keep from crying out. I begged in silence for a quick death. My thoughts scrambled until one thought eclipsed all others.

They're studying me.

I finally understood. I might not be dead yet. I might not be one of them. But they smelled the sickness in me, which meant my little attempt to save my life failed. Death approached. To them, I was no longer food for their unending hunger.

THE DEAD Vs THE DEAD

The beasts slunk off of me, but the herd hovered close by. I couldn't see them all, but they paced all around, no longer taking an interest in me. Their hissing and gnashing teeth drowned out my own thoughts. I covered my ears but couldn't block out their cries of hunger.

I allowed my head to drop against my chest and chuckled silently.

There was nothing left to do but find my gun and end this. I would never become like them. I would go out on my terms. John Taylor would never become a walking maggot fest. One bullet through my brain would ensure that.

***

The sun peaked over the rolling hills off to the west, its glowing rays rising high into the morning sky. A warm breeze brushed away the gray mist settling over the rolling fields in the final hours before daybreak. Birds started to awaken, welcoming the new day with their cheerful songs. The loud buzzing of tree beetles eclipsed most other morning chatter. Like I said, they knew nothing of the suffering we humans faced in this world overcome by the sickness.

The only other sound was my own heavy, labored breathing, each gasp barely enough to move air in and out of my lungs. My heartbeat slowed. I heard each beat grow weaker and farther and farther apart. It was like a clock with a dying battery ticking away my last few minutes. My limbs were numb and stiff as if turning to stone. My fingers struggled to tighten around the trigger of my gun. I'd finally found the fucking thing and my knife in the grass hours ago, but I still hadn't done what I knew had to be done. You can't wait any longer. My hands shook in protest, but I lifted the barrel to my head.

I was nothing more than a shell… a shell with a craving for living flesh. Drool slid down my chin. *I… hunger.*

No!

God help me. Try and hold on. I could no longer remember my wife's name, my kids' names. I couldn't even remember their faces. No, I didn't want to lose them again. *I… hunger. Pieces of my life were quickly fading away. I… need… flesh. Wait, my name— what is my name? Joh… What the hell is it? I don't know my own name. I have to kill myself now. Must… feed. What am I waiting for? Do it. Pull the damn trigger. Stop being a coward.*

I coughed and green phlegm exploded from my mouth onto my shirt. I held the barrel to my head. Still, I didn't fire.

My back leaned against the tree trunk where I'd stayed all night. Long before the first signs of morning light, the stinking undead herd had left me alone to die in peace. Under remnants of the dark skies, I stared at the gun. *Just do it!*

I coughed again and blood flew from my mouth, splattering over my arms. Feed. "No, fuck… me!"

This was it.

I had to end this suffering. Did I ever have a family? Did I have a life? I didn't know anymore. There was nothing but a black void, and hunger, in place of memories.

I gazed up one more time at the countryside. My vision was blurry. The color was gone. Nothing but gray surrounded me.

"Do… it… now!"

My finger tightened against the trigger. I closed my eyes. I painfully inhaled. Then…

A scream cut across the land.

Where had it come from?

More screaming echoed around me.

"Mommy!" a child cried. The sound was warbled, as if I was hearing it underwater, but it had come from behind me.

"I'm sorry, baby," a woman answered. "Close your eyes. Don't look at them." Again, it was little more than mumbling interrupting my final moments. Maybe it wasn't even real. Maybe the voices were in my head from some past I could no longer remember. But it seemed real, and it seemed nearby.

Then came the hissing of the Undeads.

"Get away from her, you bastard," the woman shouted.

With legs more like stone than flesh, I stiffly, painfully climbed to my feet. My head was too heavy for my neck to support. My chin drooped against my chest. Coughing and panting, I forced in just a few more crusty, fiery gulps of air.

I slowly turned around to peer through the trees, but my vision tunneled in on itself—the world narrowing into a gray, colorless vacuum tinged by blackness on all sides.

But, there was movement up ahead and more screams.

THE DEAD Vs THE DEAD

I stumbled forward, revolver still held stiffly in my hand. I was vaguely aware of holding a knife in my other hand. I just wanted to lie down in the grass. *So tired. So very, very tired.* Invisible hands strangled my neck, cutting off my air, squeezing the life out of me. My heart cried out in agony for oxygen, but there wasn't any left.

Still, I limped toward the noise.

I saw them ahead.

As if scanning the scene with out-of-focus binoculars, I spotted a woman fighting off a herd of corpses. A little girl clung to her leg.

The woman clutched two of the Undeads by their necks, trying to hold them off, but the beasts would soon feast. My mouth watered. Part of me wanted to feed as much as those beasts.

I gazed at the revolver loaded with only two rounds. If I fired, there'd be nothing left for me. My fate would be sealed. If I turned the gun on myself, the woman and child would certainly be ripped apart.

My eyes were dimming. The gray world in front of me was slipping into a blackened realm of nothingness. My body trembled uncontrollably, but I lifted my quivering hand and tried to steady the revolver's barrel.

My choice was clear.

Maybe I was more than just a rat.

The woman and child screamed.

"Get… down," I blurted, but I no longer heard my voice. The words were little more than a guttural whisper, but it was enough.

The woman peered back at me, let go of the beasts and covered her daughter with her body. I squeezed the trigger, and a round nearly blew the head off one of the Undeads. Without hesitation, I fired my only other round, which smashed into the skull of the second one, jarring his head backward. Both beasts collapsed to the earth.

The woman grabbed the child's hand and ran toward me. I couldn't make out their faces. They were just two shadowy figures.

"Thank you," the woman uttered.

"Just… run," I whispered. More drool spilled from my mouth. If she stayed, I'd… kill her… and her child. "I… will… hold… them… off."

They backed away from me, the woman shaking her head, then she scooped up the child and ran. I turned toward the approaching herd. I would soon be one of them. Nothing would prevent that now, but with my last gasp, I whispered, "Fuck… you."

I threw myself at them, slashing with my knife over and over, cutting through flesh and bone until my eyes saw nothing but blackness… until I heard the last undead hiss… until I couldn't feel anything anymore.

Until there was nothing left of me, and I slipped away into the forever shadows.

*****

Images of my wife and children flickered across my mind, like a light blinking on and off. *Come on, remember them*. For an instant I saw them clearly, just like they were in the before times, like seeing them on a movie screen. They were… perfect.

Then, my eyes fluttered open, and they were gone again.

I gazed up at a gloomy sky filled with patches of gray clouds. I lay in a grassy field, the same one where… where I'd died. But the land was cast in a shadow, dim and sad. Where the hell was I? I'd died, right? How was it possible for me to see anything? And why didn't I feel pain anymore?

Wait a second.

I didn't feel anything at all. Not my limbs, nor the pounding of my heart. I no longer had that bizarre craving for human flesh. In fact, I had no sense of hunger or thirst. I had no physical sensation of any kind, but I had emotions—and memories.

I could remember everything again. My wife's soft face and golden skin. How her crystal blue eyes glimmered when she looked at me. The way her lips felt against mine. My children's names, and the joy their laughter brought me. And I remembered their screams when they were killed. I remembered it all— the good times and the beginning of the end when the sickness took everything.

And I remembered my name.

I uttered it. "John Taylor."

I blinked my eyes and rose up on my elbows. "What's going—"

The familiar groaning of a walking corpse filled my ears.

I quickly stood and swung around. My eyes bulged, and I nearly lost my balance. The beast was… me.

THE DEAD Vs THE DEAD

The creature stood just a few feet away, seemingly unaware of my presence. Its head was arched backward as if its neck had broken. Black ooze dribbled from between its lips. Lifting a hand to my mouth, I studied the poor thing. It had my face only the skin was shredded and pale, and the pupils of its eyes were gray, just as lifeless as every other corpse. Its teeth gnashed, and its blackened tongue licked at the air. More ooze poured from its mouth.

I slowly stepped toward the beast. It just stood there, its body rigid, fingers twisted unnaturally. It moaned as if lost and alone.

Still, the beast took no notice of me.

For reasons I couldn't explain, I reached toward the creature to wrap my arms around it as if an embrace might somehow comfort it... or me. My arms passed right through it, and for the first time I noticed my own skin was more transparent than actual flesh. I lifted my hand to my face. It gave off a soft yellow glow.

I truly was... dead.

A hand grasped my shoulder. I spun around, knocking it away. "Get off of me!"

"Wait, friend, it's okay."

There, standing in front of me, was a man I'd never seen before. Behind him were a dozen other people, men, women and even some children all as transparent as me. Their skin glowed like mine. They stood in silence in this murky place, arms at their sides, unmoving, their unblinking eyes boring through me.

Behind them, visible through their ghostly forms, was a herd of Undeads.

"You are safe, friend." The man closest to me couldn't have been much older than me. Maybe he was younger. But, he spoke in a grandfatherly kind of way. His long brown hair flowed over his face, covering one eye. The other one, hazel and bright, seemed to welcome me. He wore a white-collared shirt and slacks, like some businessman or something. He tilted his head to one side, and his lips raised in a partial smile.

I balled my hands into fists. "Yeah, I'm safe? Who the hell are you? Who are they?" I nodded to the rest of the apparitions.

The man offered his hand to me. I didn't take it. "I'm Ely. And I'm like you—I guess you'd call us ghosts." He turned to the others. "And they are just like you and me. And that's all you really need to know, friend. Like you, we're all dead."

I lowered my hands. "Then are we in hell?"

Ely frowned. He brushed the hair out of his face. "In a way, yes. In life we were all overcome by the sickness, whether the disease just naturally spread to us, or we were killed by others who had already transitioned. What we all found out, just like you will learn, is that those killed by the sickness who become the Undeads are doomed to walk in this mirror version of the world."

He stopped and gazed skyward before continuing. "Maybe this is some kind of purgatory where we forever walk beside our undead corpses who exist in the real world, watching them as if watching a movie but never able to stop them. We remain tied to them until the living bash in their brains, stab them in the head or put a bullet through their skulls. When that happens, we're freed to whatever comes next. But until that happens, we can do nothing as our corpses kill over and over, spreading the sickness, sending more of the living to this… dismal realm."

Ely's face was grim. "You don't yet know the pain of watching yourself feed on the living, destroying innocent lives unable to stop yourself." He took a long breath and his chin quivered. "I am sorry to say you will know that pain and probably soon."

I shook my head. "I… I don't understand. If we're… ghosts, why did I feel your hand on my shoulder? Why are we standing here? Why aren't we just floating in some void?"

Ely scratched his chin as if to stop the trembling and compose himself. "These are good questions. I don't have all the answers. Near as I can tell, in this shadowy layer, our ethereal bodies have a kind of physicality. But, in the world of the living where our corpses exist, we do not."

I studied my glowing hands. "Why don't you just leave? You all have legs. Shit, maybe you have wings. Just go. Why stay with your walking worm-feasts? Why watch them kill?"

Ely swung to the others. "Did you hear that? He's asking why we don't just leave." The others laughed eerily.

He turned back to me. "Sorry, friend, but every one of us has asked that same question. Don't you think we've tried? It's like an invisible chain. We venture too far from our bodies and somehow, we are yanked back. There's no escape. No real hope until, like I said, the living destroy what remains of our brains."

From behind me, my corpse hissed, then began lumbering forward toward the herd as if to join the others. I watched myself stumble on shaky legs, my head still tilted backward, my eyes staring blankly at the sky.

Ely watched my body slip past us. "You know, friend, we saw what you did, sacrificing your chance at peace to save the woman and child. You should know, not only did you save them, but you saved some of us as well when in your dying moments you cut through the brains of six of our herd. You set them free. We saw the moment of peace in their eyes before they vanished into the beyond."

I huffed. "What, you mean heaven?"

Ely rubbed his hands together. "Maybe. I hope to find out one day. I hope we'll I'll have that chance to cross over to that better place."

I slumped into the grass. "Or a worse place. I mean how do we know what's out there? Can there really be a heaven? Any God that would condemn us to this hell on

Earth… well, there might be nothing else out there but more pain and suffering."

Ely sat cross-legged beside me. "I choose to have hope, and I think there's hope for you, too."

"Oh really, you don't know what I've done."

Ely placed his hand on mine. "I believe you have a good heart. Why else would you have done what you did for that woman and child?"

I lowered my head to my chest. "I… I just don't know."

Ely closed his eyes, then slowly opened them. "Friend, we've all questioned why this happened? We all fear what awaits us should we ever be freed from this… reality. We have no choice, but—"

A new thought filled my mind. "Hey, Ely, my wife and children were killed by these undead fuckers, so they must be trapped here as well. Don't suppose they're with you?"

He scanned the other glowing beings. "I don't think so. If they were, they'd already have come forward, I imagine."

I stood and grabbed him by the collar, dragging him to his feet. "You have to help me find them, Ely. I want to be reunited with them."

THE DEAD Vs THE DEAD

He nodded and raised an eyebrow. "Friend, we all want to be reunited with our families, but I don't think it works that way."

I smashed a fist into my other hand. "I have to try."

Ely put his hands on my shoulders. "I understand how you feel more than you know, and we can try to help you."

I pushed him away. I could hear in his voice he was simply telling me what I wanted to hear, but I didn't care. There had to be a way. There had to be more to death than watching my corpse feast on the living.

Ely approached me again. "Friend, I have more to say, so please listen to me."

"What else is there?"

He folded his glowing arms over his chest. "We've waited far too long for the living to find a way to stop the sickness and end this suffering, but they've failed so far. The human race is dying, and if the living can't save it, then, friend, it's up to us. We do not have our bodies, but for whatever reason, we can still think. We have to find a cure. We have to save the living if they cannot save us. And someone like you, someone with a fighting spirit, can help us."

"Sure, Ely." I walked away from him toward my corpse, which had joined the herd. They lumbered aimlessly through the tall grass in circles with no direction, no idea where to go to satisfy their need for human flesh.

There was sorrow in their groaning. I was sure of it.

Ely walked beside me. He kept his eyes on the dead. He pointed to one of them more skeletal than flesh, its ribcage exposed, its intestines hanging loosely from its waist. "You see that one. That's me. That's what the sickness turned me into. Somewhere, I have a wife and daughter and parents. I have no idea whether they are living or dead, and I can never find out because I'm trapped in here, forever tied to that… that… thing that used to be me. You see, what choice is there, friend, but to do something. How much more suffering do we—and the living—have to face."

I sighed heavily and turned to him. "What do you think we can do? We're fucking dead."

A smile returned to his face. "Why don't we find out together. Let's use what this mirror reality has to offer and find a way to destroy these corpses, end the sickness and save the world."

I clasped my hands under my chin. I gazed at my mindless raggedy, broken corpse one more time hissing and gnashing its teeth. Maybe in my death, I could be more than just a rat out to survive. "The dead versus the dead, huh? Okay, let's get to work."

Everybody Has a Poison

Heart

Shawn D. Brink

A botched lab study was to blame. It all started with just one tainted vaccine injected into some poor sucker. From there the sickness spread like wildfire.

Symptoms included aggressive behavior, irrational thoughts, degeneration of living tissue, mental instability, and a desire to bite those not yet infected. Once bitten, the victim turned in a matter of days, becoming a "poison heart". No one knows who first coined that term, but the media grabbed onto it with an iron fist.

Ramone watched this particular poison heart lumber toward him, gnashing its teeth, and salivating all over its dirty blouse. He found it difficult to look at the thing because he remembered who it used to be – who she used to be.

"Mom," he pleaded. "Don't do this, not to your only son!"

The poison heart that once was his mother didn't respond. Ramone hoped that some vestige of mercy still lingered deep within that diseased mind. But as he witnessed the emptiness in her bloodshot eyes, he knew no mercy existed.

Ramone had made a mistake. He'd fallen asleep in a dead-end alleyway, and now the thing that used to be Mother was blocking his escape.

He and his mom had survived this long by keeping an eye out for each other. Three days ago though, Ramone neglected his duty for just a moment, and Mom paid the price.

From that point on, there was nothing to do but wait. Ramone knew she'd turn. They always did. Yet, despite her pleas, he couldn't bring himself to abandon her. She was all he had left.

He'd planned to leave just before she would turn. That was a risky game, but this was his mother. He just couldn't bring himself to leave her until the end. She deserved to be in the company of her only son until then.

EVERYONE HAS A POISON HEART

The problem with Ramone's strategy was that he required sleep. He'd tried to stay awake. He'd tried to remain vigilant. But she'd turned when he was catching a cat nap, which is how he ended up trapped in a dead-end alleyway with a poison heart closing in.

"Come here. Come to Mommy," it said with raspy voice.

Ramone didn't respond. This wasn't his mother speaking, but only the poison heart she'd become. He couldn't let it get into his head.

The poison heart moved forward and Ramone backed up until his shoulder blades pressed against the old brown-brick building at the end of the alley. As it drew nearer, he jumped and grabbed the bottom rung of the fire escape ladder that was above him. He clamored up the ladder as the creature lashed out with gnarled hands. Fortunately, Ramone rose above its reach just in the nick of time.

He collapsed onto the 2nd story platform, too exhausted and sorrowful to go further. He sprawled out onto his stomach, staring at the creature through the steel grating of the platform floor.

SHAWN D. BRINK

The poison heart looked up at Ramone with rage-filled eyes. Those eyes told the whole story. It wanted him. It desired him. It wanted just one good bite.

It tried to climb the ladder, but Ramone didn't move from his spot. He knew the creature lacked the coordination skills to climb. It was a known fact in this strange new world.

After a few failed attempts, it resorted to a tantrum of sorts, swinging its arms about and wailing like a banshee.

Ramone watched for a bit, but soon grew bored. He rolled over and stared up at the sky. It was overcast, like his mood.

Ramone wished he had his bat. Unfortunately, he'd left it in the alley. He could see it in the distance, near the end of the alley – so close, yet unretrievable.

That bat was his prized possession, a Louisville Slugger that he'd gotten for his 15th birthday. Back then, before the world turned on its ear, it worked well for hitting homeruns. These days, he used it for smashing in poison hearts' skulls.

Below, he could hear the thing that was once his mother. "Help me son," it said.

EVERYONE HAS A POISON HEART

"Mother is down here. It's not safe. Please, help me up."

Ramone knew better. He remained unmoving, staring up, looking into the cloudy sky. He thought back to his pre-pandemic life. He'd been working a dead-end job. His band was on hiatus. His father was dead. His mother, bless her heart, was doing the best she could raising a son in the city as a single mother on a limited income.

Back then, he'd thought of his life as one giant turd ball. If he had only known then what he knew now – well, his attitude would have been much different.

Maybe it wouldn't be so bad.

He shivered as that thought entered his mind.

Maybe it would be better just to let her bite me.

He wanted to undo that line of thinking, but it stuck like glue.

It would only suck until I turn, then I probably wouldn't care much.

He rolled over and looked at the creature that used to be Mom. It stared back, grinding its teeth.

Maybe it wouldn't be so bad to become a poison heart – to lose my sorrow, my pain, myself. To become oblivious to everything I once was, everything I had been – everything I could become.

"Ramone," it called to him through clenched jaws. "Why don't you come down here and spend some time with your mom?"

"You'll bite me," he answered.

"I won't. I promise."

Ramone ignored the lie. "Will you at least do it quickly?"

Something akin to a smile grew on the creature's face. It nodded.

"Will it hurt?"

It shook its head. "Just for a moment. Just a quick pinch. That's all. Just a quick pinch."

Ramone sighed. *Just a quick pinch and all the crap disappears. That doesn't sound too bad.*

The thing licked its lips. "It will be like pulling a bandage from a wound. I'll do it quickly, and then it'll be done.

Ramone put his right foot on the highest rung of the ladde. "I'm tired of running."

"Yes," it said. "Once you turn, you'll be in a whole new world. It will be grand. No more running."

He put his left foot on the top rung beside the right and held the railing tight with his clenched fists. He tried to climb down, but his body didn't move. The instinct of self-preservation was clinging to him like a vicious parasite.

Below, the thing that was once Mother raised blue-veined arms toward Ramone, as if he were a nervous kid preparing to go down a slide at the park. Those arms disgusted him. They were blistered and weeping. They were not his mother's arms.

"Come to Mother," it said. "Mother knows how to make it all better."

Ramone's knees shook as he stood there on that first rung, holding onto the railing for balance. Below, the creature began to tremble excitedly.

"Come to Mommy, Ramone. Helpless child, come to Mommy."

Ramone's breathing became loud, almost wheezy. This was harder than he'd thought it would be. *Let go of the railing idiot! No reason to hang around. Everyone you care about is gone, might as well join them.*

Its tongue licked its lips as a fresh coat of pink saliva drooled down its chin. Something akin to a purr escaped its throat.

"I want to forget everything," Ramone blurted.

"Yes! You will forget it all! Now come!"

Ramone closed his eyes. He let one foot dangle free from the security of the ladder.

"Jump!" he heard it squeal. "I'll catch you, my son!"

He shouted down. "I don't want to remember anything!"

"You won't! I promise!"

With his eyes remaining shut, Ramone let go of the railing and allowed himself to fall away from the ladder. It was a strange exhilaration.

"Come here, Ramo..." Its voice was cut short by a loud boom. A millisecond later, he landed and opened his eyes.

The thing that was once his mother had broken his fall. It didn't grab him. It didn't bite him. It couldn't bite him, not with its head missing.

EVERYONE HAS A POISON HEART

He rolled away from the decapitated creature and scrambled to his feet. Brains, blood, and other assorted bits were splattered everywhere.

"Are you okay?" Someone asked.

Ramone looked up from the dead thing at his feet. She stood about four yards from him, holding a shotgun with smoke wafting from the barrel. Her head was cocked slightly. A curious expression covered her face.

He guessed her to be in her early twenties. She was wearing a black-leather jacket. The jacket was undone, revealing a bright pink T-shirt. She wore black denim jeans with torn out knees. On her feet were a dirty pair of pink Chuck Taylors.

Her spiked hair matched the color of her shoes and shirt, but what drew Ramone's attention, besides the fact that her gun was aimed at his face, was the earring in her left ear. It was an oversized silver cross which dangled all the way from her earlobe to the top of her shoulder.

"Are you okay?" she repeated. "If you've been bitten, you should let me know so that I can blow your head off too. It'll be better for both of us that way."

He answered meekly. "I haven't been bitten."

"If you're lying, I'll know."

"I have not been bitten!" Ramone answered, this time with conviction.

"What in the world were you doing?" she hissed as she lowered her weapon. "Do you have a death wish or something?"

Ramone answered. "I was tired of running."

"Why?"

"There's nobody left but poison hearts."

"That's crazy." She lowered her weapon. "There's a whole camp of us just outside the city. There's hundreds of us."

"Are you for real?" Ramone wondered.

"Of course I'm for real." She rolled her eyes. "The name's Sheena."

"I'm Ramone. What are you doing here?"

"Searching for survivors. Now, come with me if you want to live."

Ramone looked once more at the headless creature near his feet. "That was my mother."

Sheena sighed. "I'm sorry." The distant howl of a poison heart echoed from somewhere beyond the alley. "We can't stick around, not with all the commotion we've caused. "They'll be here any second. We've got to leave now!"

He retrieved his bat from the end of the alley and went with her. "You know," he said as they walked along. "Until you showed up, I really thought I was the only one left."

She nodded. "I used to think the same thing once upon a time, before I found the others. Things got pretty dark for me back then when I was all alone."

"Did you ever consider – you know, doing what I almost did?" he asked.

"You mean, just letting them take me?"

Sheena stopped and turned toward him. She looked into his eyes and he could tell she'd been through hell. "Yeah, I used to want that in the worst way. I almost let it happen on multiple occasions. Still not sure what kept me from letting it happen." Then she pointed at her earring. "But I don't want to do that anymore because I've found my strength."

"Strength? What strength?" Ramone was intrigued.

Sheena just smiled as that cross glimmered in the gloomy light of the cloudy day. "Come with me and I'll tell you all about it."

SHAWN D. BRINK
THE END

The Nightmare Tree

Shawn D. Brink

Levi ran by the red-flannelled scarecrow in the cornfield's middle. He bolted by it quickly. He didn't like the scarecrow. Its black-button eyes creeped him out.

He arrived at the trees which grew up along the far side of the field. Only the scarecrow's head was visible from here, just a pinprick dot in the green vastness of the field. Six-foot-tall cornstalks hid the rest of it.

The scarecrow was too far away now for Levi to see those black-button eyes. The thought of them though made him uneasy.

Looking beyond the scarecrow and the field, he could just barely make out the top of Uncle John's two-story farmhouse. It looked so distant from his perspective with that high sea of corn between.

He turned toward the trees. He loved to climb and even had a treehouse of his own back home in Omaha, Nebraska. Here there were not tree houses, just many places from which to hang and dangle.

He walked along that narrow space between the corn and the trees. Here, the dense foliage made everything dim – well, not everything. He spied a bright spot ahead.

Levi entered the bright spot. Here no leaves blocked the sun. Directly before him, like a monolith, stood a massive dead cottonwood. Its sun-bleached branches rose toward the sky, leafless.

Levi shivered despite summer's heat. Seeing that tree reminded him of Halloween and the chill of October winds.

"Howdy."

Levi jumped.

The voice had come from above. He looked up and saw somebody sitting in the dead tree, their legs dangling freely from one of the main branches.

The boy appeared to be about Levi's age. He was wearing a pair of worn denim overalls with no shirt beneath. The unruly mop of orange hair on the boy's head made Levi think of a troll doll.

"You're not from around here are ya?" said the kid.

THE NIGHTMARE TREE

"No. I'm visiting my Uncle. I'm from Omaha." Levi added, "This is my uncle's field."

"Don't mean to be tresspasin' or nothing," the boy said. "But this here tree is a great specimen don't you think?"

"I guess," Levi answered.

"Do you like climbing?"

"Sure."

The kid smiled. "Well, what're you waiting for?"

"Is it safe?" It certainly didn't look safe.

"I'm in it ain't I?"

"It looks dead."

"It just looks dead because it's The Nightmare Tree."

Levi's skin prickled. "What?"

"Never fall asleep under The Nightmare Tree. If you do, you got to get home before the scarecrow gets you." The kid grinned as he watched Levi's reaction. "You ain't scared, are ya?"

"No," Levi lied.

"Good. Let's climb."

And with that, Levi ascended the tree.

"Wanna play a game?" the boy asked.

"Okay."

"Ever play tree tag?"

Levi shook his head.

"It's just like regular tag except you got to stay in the tree. I'll count to ten so you can get a head start. Then, I'll come after ya. One—two—three—."

Levi started climbing. The boy was right. The tree looked dead, but in reality, it seemed quite strong.

"Four—five—six—seven—."

Levi crept higher, trying to scout out the best limbs for tag-evasion.

"Eight—nine—ten. Ready or not, here I come." The boy approached, looking very cat-like as he slunk nearer and nearer to where Levi perched.

Levi realized he'd climbed himself into a corner. "I give up."

"You can't give up until you're tagged." The boy responded as he reached out his hand.

Before the tag came though, Levi heard a loud crack followed by a sickening sensation. He barely had time to realize the cracking sound was of his branch breaking and the sensation was that of him falling.

Pain wracked his whole body as he landed on the hard-packed ground. He tried to catch his breath, but his lungs seemed unwilling to inhale.

Everything started spinning. Levi tried to sit up, but it was no use.

You should never fall asleep under The Nightmare Tree, he recalled just as everything went dark.

***

Levi opened his eyes. High above, a single pale eye watched him. *No,* he thought. *Not an eye. It's the moon.*

The moon looked fractured, as if it had been dropped and then poorly glued back together. His eyes came into focus and he realized the fractured moon was an optical illusion created by the fact he was looking at it through the bare branches of The Nightmare Tree. *You should never fall asleep under The Nightmare Tree.*

"The boy awakes!"

That voice unnerved Levi. He staggered to his feet and spun toward it.

It was the kid, but he looked different under the moonbeams. He was peeking out at Levi from behind The Nightmare Tree's trunk.

"You shouldn't have fallen asleep under the Nightmare Tree!" the boy hissed.

The boy glowed in the moonlight. His appearance reminded Levi of the dangly phosphorescent lures deep-sea fishes have attached to their heads to attract prey.

The boy laughed sadistically. "Better get home before you-know-who gets you."

Levi bolted into the cornfield. His only thought was to get home by the most direct route.

"Beware the scarecrow! Beware the scarecrow!" He heard the boy's voice from behind.

Levi reached the middle of the cornfield, but the scarecrow wasn't on his perch. All that remained was the pine post on which the scarecrow had once been attached.

Somewhere in the unseen distance, Levi heard a sloshy, sloppy sound. He glanced back, but the cornstalks blocked his view. In his imagination's eye though, he could see the scarecrow coming fast, sprinting through the mud like a bull seeing red.

Levi ran like a maniac, feeling the broad leaves of the corn cut his face and arms. He burst from the corn and entered the farmyard. The house was directly before him.

He glanced back, and there was the scarecrow. It flew from the cornfield, shrieking like a banshee. Those black-button eyes now glowed red with hellfire.

Levi tripped over something in the darkness and hit his chest on the lowest porch step. He cried out, sure he'd cracked a rib.

He tried to get up, but before he could, the scarecrow fell upon him, weightier than what straw, burlap, and flannel could account for. It pulled him off the porch steps, back on the yard.

Levi kicked at it, screaming the entire time. A straw-hand wrapped around his leg. Burlap teeth sank into the flesh of his heel.

The pain was excruciating. In horror, he looked at the scarecrow as it chomped down again, tearing all the way to the bone.

Never fall asleep under The Nightmare Tree! If you do, you got to get home before the scarecrow gets you!

Levi grabbed at the porch stairs railing. He gripped it and pulled himself more fully onto the porch.

The scarecrow remained attached to his dangling foot like a hungry shark. Levi shook his leg, but the creature only sunk its teeth deeper.

He pulled on the railing yet again and gained another step. Now only his mangled foot remained off the porch.

"You fell asleep under the Nightmare Tree," mumbled the scarecrow through its flesh-filled burlap cheeks. "You belong to me!"

Levi screamed and pulled once more with all he had.

***

Bright light blinded Levi. He lashed out, clawing at anything in reach.

"Ouch! Stop it, Levi! It's just me!"

Despite the sunlight blazing through the bare branches of The Nightmare Tree, Levi could make out Uncle John's silhouette.

"Don't move," John said. "You must have fallen from the tree. Your leg's pretty messed up."

"Where's the boy?" Levi screamed.

"What boy?"

THE NIGHTMARE TREE

Levi didn't answer. What could he say? *The one that serves as the tree's lure just as deep sea predators have their luminescent lures dangling before their gaping maws?*

"We need to get you to a doctor."

John broke off one of The Nightmare Tree's limbs and used it as a splint, securing it to Levi's leg with his shirt.

Uncle John lifted Levi and carried him off through the cornfield. As they passed the middle of the field, Levi couldn't help but look toward where the pine post stood.

There hung the scarecrow, as if all was right as rain. Its burlap head was tilted toward them. Those black-button eyes watched silently.

Then the corn hid it from Levi's sight.

Jill's Visitor

Shawn D. Brink

A six-inch piece of intestine bulged through a laceration in Jill's gut. *It looks like a gray sausage in a pool of marinara sauce,* she thought to herself.

The collision was a bad one. Jill glanced at her bicycle. It was barely visible. Most of it was under the sedan that ran the red light and used her for a speed bump.

She tried to sit up, but firm hands forced her back. "Don't move, not until we access your injuries."

She looked up. Three people stood over her. Two were paramedics. The third was a police officer.

"Can you tell me your name?" the officer asked.

"Jill."

The paramedics worked quickly and within moments, the sterile environment of an ambulance replaced that of the accident. The doors slammed shut. The siren began to scream.

And just like that, Jill was whisked away from the accident scene.

One of the paramedics sat with her in the back, checking her vitals. "Jill, you are a very lucky girl. Things could have been much…"

"Ryan, can you please come up here," the driver's voice came over a static-ridden intercom.

"I've got to go for just a moment," paramedic Ryan said before he left her alone in the back of the ambulance.

Laying upon the stretcher, she looked down at her lacerated gut. It was a ghastly sight.

"It doesn't hurt because you're in shock, in case you're wondering."

Jill looked toward the voice. Beside her sat another. He wore denim jeans and a black hooded sweatshirt with the hood up.

"Who are you?"

Saying nothing, he pulled his hood back.

A chill washed over her as she beheld that face. She'd seen him before in pictures. Although, here in the back of the ambulance, he lacked the sickle and cloak that so often accompanied him in artist renditions.

"I suppose you know why I'm here," Death said with a cruel grin.

Tears formed in the corners of her eyes. "No, this is a mistake," she said with little more than a squeak.

"If I had a dead man's dollar for every time I heard that one."

She struggled to find her voice. "Honestly, I'm not dying. This is all just an act."

Death leaned back. "It is?" He sounded amused.

"My older brother, he's a cop..."

"Jill," he interrupted with a scoff. "That fact might help you out of speeding tickets, but it doesn't allow you to cheat death."

"He asked me to participate in this drill..."

"A drill huh?" he interrupted again. "Ok, I'll entertain your objection. Tell me why I am mistaken, Jill. Tell me why you are not dying."

Jill's heart quickened as she formed her defense. "The city organized this mock car accident as a training exercise. They wanted to see how all the departments and agencies worked together in such a situation. They hoped to find ways to improve response time, increase lines of communication, that sort of thing."

"I don't know anything about that," Death said matter-of-factly. "All I know is that my list for today has your name on it. That means it's time for you to stand before God for judgement. I never come by mistake."

"Well, there's a first time for everything," she responded. "Because I'm just a volunteer in a fake accident."

Death remained silent.

"Let me prove it to you."

Death grinned from ear to ear. "You can try, but I don't think you'll succeed."

Jill reached down to her abdominal injury. She grabbed. She yanked.

Death watched. His smile disappeared.

"You see? It's just latex and catsup," she said as she dangled the rubbery appendage before his eyes.

Death stared at the prop and rubbed his chin. "Well, I'll be."

"How's that for proof?" she pressed.

"I'm impressed Jill. This has never happened before."

JILL'S VISITOR

"So go away, and don't come back until I am really dying, preferably in about a hundred years."

Death stood up, replaced his hood and stepped right through the ambulance wall. But just as he exited, the combined screech of tires on asphalt, metal grinding against metal, and screams coming from the cab, bombarded the scene.

I never come by mistake.

Death's words reverberated in her mind as the ambulance flipped onto its side. Quick as lightning, his hand reached back through the ambulance wall and grabbed her securely. "It's time to go, Jill my girl. The judge is waiting."

The Only Road Home

Francesca Quarto

She believed she was invincible. The goddess had given her that impression after all.

"Here, take this stone and you shall prevail," she had told her cunningly.

But goddesses have been known to manipulate the truth to suit their own ends. Was this to prove one of those times? Her life depended upon the answer.

Clutching the smooth gray rock, she stepped out of the shadows where she'd hidden, waiting for the moon to be lost beneath the storm-heavy clouds. She let the darkness engulf her like a wave, not moving so much as a flutter of eyelids. Dressed in the black robes of the Acolyte, its hood concealing the glossy mass of coppery red hair, she melted into the night.

A low rumble, like snow gathering into the teeth of an avalanche, began to ride the incessant winds. It grew louder, overwhelming all other senses until it filled her head. She fought the urge to reach up to cover her ears. Behind the churning sound came the thud and tramp of heavy footsteps. The weight they carried surely crushed the very earth beneath, marking it forever with its passage. The moon hung desolate and alone under its mask of inky thunder heads, waiting and watching just as she did.

The goddess had only relinquished the stone after she had proven herself the Acolyte of Merit; the one chosen for this delicate mission. Though she understood this was an undertaking from which she might never return, she believed it defined her very existence. She, and the others of her kind, named the *Original Sinners*, had been locked away on this bleak and dying world, for crimes committed by faceless, nameless ancestors. The Ancient's outrage was deemed so great by the gods, that any of their progeny would also suffer their fate. Of these, only a handful remained.

Late, in the blast of the red summer, she had become the last female. There were now only six of the *Original Sinners* left to roam the barren wastes of their dark prison world. The others, all madmen without conscience or pride, stalked her like the sexual prey they viewed her to be.   The goddess only intervened because she was bored watching the same game of hide and seek, day after night.

Her instructions to the girl were easy enough, "Follow the path that shall be revealed to you by the stone's light."

She was gripping the hard edges of her gift, until they pressed painfully into her palm. She wondered how its dull surface could ever show the way to the only road home; back to a place of light and life. The path back was through this narrow gap of time.

The sound of a low growl, like a stomach crying out to be filled, another heavy thump upon the parched, dead ground...Here he comes. She tossed the stone ahead of her so she could follow it to freedom. It made a shallow sound as it skipped like a rock over the flat face of a pond. But there were no tranquil ponds here, only brackish waters to quench a burning thirst.

It stopped several yards in front of her. She stood mutely rooted to the spot, waiting for the light. Suddenly, a shimmer of yellow began to pool around the tossed stone. The glow began to seep into the desiccated ground and shot back out like a bolt of lightning in reverse. This was the road home, illuminated for her at last.

Breaking her statue like stillness, she began to sprint like the fabled hart, to wherever this road would lead. I am going home, she kept thinking, as she pumped her legs and panted her breath into the eternal night.

The goddess watched from her marble throne as the creature ran into the oblivion of imagination. It still shone with the intensity of belief, beckoned with a voracity of freedom, but sadly, was only the mirage of a path out of her current existence. It was only a stone after all, not a gem. She had taken it, even knowing at face value, it was nothing but a stone. Smooth to the touch, sounding of promise when it was tossed, but still, only a rock.

"Ah, how silly these humans can be. They chase after illusion every time," she sighed to the scudding clouds over her marble head.

Her hands lay upon her knees, each palm up. One held a precious gem, the other, empty. Not unlike the promise of the stone the girl had chosen. The goddess continued to chuckle as she watched the girl follow the promises, until she faded into the distance. The female human would know the truth in the end. There would be no road back home, but then this peculiar being seemed ever hopeful and optimistic.

"Such a waste of your limited time," she mumbled to the girl who never heard. She was too busy trying to get back to a past that didn't exist, and to live a future that was only a dream. For her part, the goddess decided to divert her attention to a new supplicant, the wandering man in the dessert. He'd been stubbornly stronger than the rest, never falling for her promises, but she could be very persuasive.

The Alien's Mother

Francesca Quarto

It was a typical Mother's Day in the small outpost of Glimmer Roost. They still celebrated long-remembered holidays from Earth times, only now, they did it in zero gravity. No bunches of roses and boxes of chocolates. Just the hand-made cards that could be erased and reused for the next holiday. There was no shortage of shiny baubles to be given, they were as common as road gravel back on Terra Uno. After all, the brilliant stones gave the very name to the mining town.

Mother's Day wasn't that big around there anyway, what with the lack of any women. And usually the only time the word "mother" was spoken, it was quickly followed with a profanity; a word likely to be around human settlements until the end days. This Mother's Day seemed destined to be marked like hundreds before it on Glimmer Roost…they broke out the Alien's Mother.

The female of her species landed on the remote planet, several months after the Pilgrim Miners. Workers living bubbles, a medical and research lab, and weigh stations for the far-flung outpost, were already installed and scattered over a large area. In a quick ceremony in the red glow of a second moonrise, the mining post was dubbed *Glimmer Roost.* The post commander figured it was shooting off the flares in celebration that caught the attention of the planetary rover.

The alien announced her arrival by blasting a group of unarmed surveyors and building engineers into space dust. There was no provocation on their part unless you count their aggressive reshaping of her planet's landscape. One particularly enormous mound was flattened early in their terra forming process. Unfortunately, as they learned later, this particular geographic feature was the alien's domicile. The hive-like structure of connecting tunnels and chambers was subsequently shattered, and buried under the weight of the debris. At the time of its destruction, the hive sheltered the Alien's entire family tree, from oldest to youngest.

THE ALIEN'S MOTHER

She responded as any mother would, with unchecked rage and righteous lethality. She entered into a running skirmish with the Pilgrim Guard Unit, called in by the lone survivor at the mound killings. Her eradication was assured. They were human mercenaries, trained in the finer points of killing an enemy. She, as they discovered, was a mother, and the last defender of what was her home planet.

The body of the alien mother was to be kept for further study by the scientists that would follow one day. She was perfectly preserved, but as time went on, the Pilgrims realized the corporation funding Glimmer Roost, would not waste resources on studying anything that couldn't produce a profit. Being human men, offspring of mothers all, they were collectively moved after the first one hundred years of keeping her in cold storage, to celebrate that most honored holiday, Mother's Day.

Forthwith, the preserved body of the alien mother was brought to the communal feasting shell, where the children of humankind, could lay hand-made gifts around her blueish feet and short, whip-like tail. They had taken this mother of another race, co-opting her as their own. Over a span of many hundred cycles, the stories, along with the petrified shell of the last mother on Glimmer Roost, was dramatically transformed. She gradually evolved from death bringer to life giver, from alien, to familiar. Mother's Day became "The Great Mother's Day," proving, even in dying, there was eternal life for the love of an Alien Mother.

The First Love Match

Francesca Quarto

"It's no matter, pet. One day you'll find yourself besieged with offers of marriage. A dear girl like you, with a heart as big as the sky above! Here, have another honey cake, dear. "

Her mother's answer to any challenge in life was a sweetie of some sort. Plagued by worries of her continued spinsterhood, Corina feared her girth might soon match her dark moods.

"Mother. I am no longer willing to sit about, waiting for a suitable man to come banging on the gate, asking for the opportunity to bring me flowers and candies and pallid conversation! I shall no longer spend my time trying to entertain braggarts, brutes and banal bumpkins!"

She stormed out of the room leaving her mother with mouth gaping, and the lady's maid snickering behind her hand.

Corina went straight to her rooms, asked a servant to bring her paper and pen, and began writing on the creamy parchment in her sharp and practiced hand.

"Seeking Gentleman for Potential Loving Relationship. My description as follows:

Highly intelligent, good wit, patient beyond sainthood, tolerable storyteller, intolerant of fools and braggarts, loving of the Creator's natural world, respectful of all persons, no matter their gender. Appearance NOT relevant...Demeanor is all. The Lazy and Arrogant need NOT apply."

Lady Corina Forthright

Handing this off to the waiting serving girl, she gave her a small coin, along with the notice, "I want you to post this in the village square, where other news items are on display."

Then Corina sat back and waited for her replies to come in.

The first, as predictable as storms in spring, came from the town dandy. A lay-about heir to a vast fortune, he was seeking a new thrill to brighten his dull days as a budding cretin. He presented himself to Corina, two of his toadies in tow, ready to praise him to the heavens if called upon as character witnesses. His puny overtures were easily deflected by the robust young woman he desperately tried to charm. Any interest faded as quickly as his perfumed wig under her scrutiny and questioning. Corina scanned his frills and curls, noting the touch of powder on a pale face that never saw a walk in a summer field. She turned on her heels, left the room and smiled to herself when she heard his gasp of disbelief.

Suitor number two was not as obviously mis-matched to this fine young lady. Sir Ralph Longstreet was a self-proclaimed intellectual, with several papers on history penned under a fictitious name, and a penchant for stirring controversy with his unpopular rants on societal woes at dinner parties. His interests, however, were narrowly defined by a rather blind egotism. He would brook no differing of opinion, as he alone held the defining one. Corina thanked him for contributing his views of the world that existed in his very small mind. She left him pacing, mid-lecture, on his unique insights regarding a woman's place as mere muse, in the world of letters.

This parade of sad excuses for a man in full, went on for nigh onto a year. The parchment fixed to the wall on the Village Square was tattered and faded and nearly illegible from the elements. Naturally, few had the gift of reading, but word circulated quickly around the countryside and beyond, of this novel effort to find a potential husband. The Lady's quest soon morphed into urban legend as the months passed like wind-driven clouds.

One day, a few days before Corina's thirty-something birthday, a caller came to the gates seeking entry at an hour still under the cloak of darkness. His insistent clamor raised half the residents within the manor; the others, being over the age of either hearing, or caring, or both. Corina was immediately roused by the clanging of the gate as it swung inward. She peered out her tall bedroom window in time to see a hunched figure ride through the gate. He swung himself from his magnificent stead with the grace of a boulder racing downhill. His arms appeared rather longish for his seemingly short stature, swinging like loose tree limbs from a stout tree.

"Oh, sweet Mother!" Corina moaned.

Feeling obligated to meet any who answered her peculiar manner of seeking a mate, she snatched a comforter off her bed. Wearing it like a queen's robes, she set her jaw for confrontation, and her heart for disappointment. She found the man installed in her smaller, intimate sitting room. The stranger had his back to her as he stood in front of a warming fireplace. Corina studied him from behind, noting the slope of his shoulders, the stubby bowed legs, and a mop of hair that sat on his head like the foam on a small beer. She cleared her throat. He turned.

She sucked in a breath when she saw his eyes were a deep red, glittering like rubies in a dead-white face. He smiled, and for a flash of a moment, his eye teeth gleamed long and sharp in his mouth. He had pushed his long cloak to his hunched back, enlarging its deformity.

"Good evening, Lady Corina."

His voice was like the feel of silk upon her skin. She gave a small shudder as she sensed, more than saw him move toward her. Suddenly they were within touching distance. He stared into her light gray eyes so intently, she nearly forgot to speak.

"You come calling at an odd hour, sir."

This sounded silly even to her ears, and she smiled back at him when he laughed.

"Yes, but this is one of my favorite times; when all is still, but the beating of our hearts."

Corina found this explanation totally logical and gestured for him to take a seat. He joined her on the brocaded love seat she favored in this room, and without asking her leave, took up her free hand, while the other clutched tightly to keep the comforter closed around her. She looked down momentarily at the long fingers and his very pallid skin. It seemed natural that he held her hand. He slowly raised his free hand to her slightly heaving breast, and then up to the pulse, hammering now, at the side of her neck, and lingered there for several heart beats.

His eyes never left Corina's during this intimate exploration. For her part, she only sighed with half-lidded eyes, at each contact of his roaming hand. The fire began to burn low by the time the stranger opened the door to the sitting room. There were no servants about at this hour, save the gatekeeper, lying iner again in his room at the back of the gate house.

They exited the murky hallway as the stranger threw open the heavy doors with a flick of his wrist. Walking silently under the velvety dome, and bathed in the moon's creamy glow, everything appeared filtered by a heavy gauze to Corina's eyes. She was aware that the stranger had a tight hold of her hand as he led her to his untethered horse. The horse snorted in recognition and the stranger patted him to silence. Turning to Corina he spoke again, his voice calm and soothing.

"I have come to claim you, dear lady. You will share all my years of living in this world. Know all that you want shall be yours, in me as my station is equal to your own."

He lifted her effortlessly, placing her gently onto his saddle, springing like a deer to sit behind her. The comforter she hung over her shoulders was long dropped away, but she felt no chill as he wrapped his long arms tightly around her, pulling her into the curve of his body.

She seemed to find her voice as they cantered out of the courtyard.

"Your station you say, is equal?   What then shall I call you sir?"

"Count will do, my dear."

Revenge of the Dragons

Elizabeth Alsobrooks

"Seeking revenge only turns you into a victim," her grandmother used to say whenever Ari complained about the many injustices taking place in the realms just beyond the meadow that separated their home from those of the humans and other warring factions.

As far as Ari could tell the humans fought most ruthlessly against each other and only bothered themselves with others if they tried to infringe on their lands. Their greatest motivator was greed. They'd been warring with each other for longer than Ari's 300 years, longer even than some of the elders who were much older than her own grandmother's 1000 years.

Ari's ancestors had once been known as woodland elves, but when humans learned to ride dragons the elves used their magic to create a realm of stone and mortar that presided over a massive dam that controlled the water flow of Mardel, a large lake basin surrounded by mountains. The woodlands of the foothills climbed all the way to the lake, so the elves still hunted their ancestral forests.

Highly skilled with a bow, Ari escaped the confines of her walled home, Arahluna, to hunt in the woods. Game was plentiful. The elven city was cloaked to outsiders and since it was known that elves, legendary practitioners of magic, roamed the forest, few humans ventured further than the outer regions. There were nearby woods in which they could hunt. Since there were no riches to be plundered in Gabernon Forest, the humans had not yet ordered their dragons to blaze the aged trees.

Gilivan pointed to the left and Ari nodded. She smelled the buck's musk on the morning breeze. Taking aim, she released her nocked arrow. Too late. Without hesitation the buck bolted over the hill and out of sight. Her arrow struck a tree behind his last location just as a dark shadow drifted overhead, so large it blocked the sun.

"Biggest one yet," Gilivan grumbled.

It was going to be a long day. Ari nodded and scrambled after her prey. The deer were now scattered to the south, far from their greatest predator, a dragon. There had been a much larger number of them this summer, which meant the humans established bloodlines capable of taming and riding dragons. The elves knew all about the dragons. The dangerous beasts would not accept just any rider. They locked eyes with any candidate and seemed to perform some sort of telepathic evaluation before they decided to accept or reject any prospective riders. If they accepted them, they formed an immediate and unbreakable bond. The rider was able to convey their wishes to the dragon telepathically, in much the same way elves could communicate with one another. With dragons, the link lasted until the rider's death. Only then would the dragon allow another rider to bond with them. Basic but true was the fact that the human faction with the most and biggest dragons wielded the greater power. Dragons made the elves prey scarcer and skittish.

Headed back with a wagonload of meat and forest herbs, Ari turned to her brother and said, "I heard the scouts say that only two factions of humans wield dragons. They say they're too evenly matched to chance attacking each other any more."

"That and there's no plunder if all you're going to get is ashes," Gilivan replied.

"Grandmother told me elves were the first dragon riders. I wonder why we stopped?"

"We didn't. The elves at Allhluna still ride dragons. Dozens of them."

"What? Why don't they ever ride them when they come here? It would be faster than horseback."

"Because there are humans on dragons here. They don't want the dragons from different bloodlines to fight for dominance, and don't want the humans to know elves ride dragons."

"I can't believe I never knew this. How did you find out?"

"My friend's dad is a general and he knew."

"How do we get to ride one?"

"Eventually we might."

Ari twisted in the seat to look her brother in the face. She managed to keep from grabbing his arm in excitement. "How? I want to do it right away!"

REVENGE OF THE DRAGONS

"I don't know if ever. I only know our family's bloodline is descended from dragon riders. There's a list in a book in the library archives and my friend said our name was on it."

"Did you ask father about it?" Ari would have immediately done so and couldn't believe her older brother hadn't.

He raised an eyebrow, pushed his shoulder-length golden hair behind a pointed ear and said, "Of course. He said I would know more when I needed to know more."

"That sounds like father."

Ari turned back to the trail and began plotting a way to convince her grandfather to tell her more. They rode at a steady incline for a few minutes, each wrapped in their own musings.

Their hunters senses pulled them from their thoughts and they turned as one to scan the landscape behind them. Gilivan pulled on the reins and halted the horses. He tied the reins to the wagon and jumped down, nodding for Ari to join him.

She barely cleared the seat when an arrow splintered the wood beside her shoulder. A quick glance before she ducked was all she needed to know the double row fletching was human in origin. She nocked an arrow in her bow, peering between the side rails of the wagon for a target.

"They're from a dragon clan," Gilivan said softly.

"I know. What are they doing this close to the city?"

"There's only one way they could know of its existence." Gilivan dodged an arrow and sent one into the chest of the man in the tree. He watched him fall screaming to the ground before Gilivan said, "We have a traitor to catch."

Ari watched as her arrow found its mark and another human fell from where he'd chanced exposing himself to attack.

They waited a few minutes, both inhaling the scents of the forest, their ears straining to hear any foreign sounds.

"They must have been scouts. Have you informed —" Hooves pounded the ground. Both siblings turned to watch as a troop of elven calvary surrounded them. A signal from a general sent a dozen riders deeper into the darkening forest to search for humans and other threats.

REVENGE OF THE DRAGONS

The general turned to Gilivan and said, "Hurry. You need to get back. Your father summoned you. Where's the rest of the hunting party?"

"After a bear," Ari said. "Our wagon was already full, so we were bringing it home."

The officer nodded and signaled for the pair to mount the wagon and head home. They quickly complied, wondering why their father summoned them. He must surely know what just occurred.

Ari entered her chamber and stopped. "This looks like more than a welcome home from a hunting trip."

"You yourself sent me a telepathic message about the attack. Did you think we'd be at ease until you returned?"

"I'm sorry we put you to so much trouble, grandmother," she said, reaching out to give her a warm embrace. Though white, her grandmother's hair was waist length and today it was braided down her back. It complimented her iridescent blue gown and her silver jewelry.

She was a lighter version of her daughter, who stood beside her, hair so blond it glowed nearly as white as her mother's. "Your bath is drawn, Ari. Hurry and bathe and get dressed. Your father sent for you," her mother said in ancient elven. That and the firm tone in her mother's voice sent Ari rushing to comply.

Trailing her mother and grandmother, Ari entered the throne room. Bright candlelight reflected off the iridescent walls and shimmered off the gilt adornments and gossamer clothing of the nobles. She paused only a moment before forcing herself to continue across the room and bow to her father. "Sire," she said softly. She knew he was speaking to her, but not even her elven hearing could make out what he said above the ringing in her ears.

It didn't matter. She knew well enough what was taking place. She'd seen it before when her brother got betrothed to his wife. She recognized her future husband too. No surprise there. Except perhaps the timing. And the pre-betrothal ceremony discussion. She had met Prince Joran of course. His smile broadened when she glanced at him, standing next to his father, King Oloren. Though she didn't dislike him, for he seemed kind and even charming if she were honest. The problem was she didn't love him and didn't want to marry anyone. Especially since no one thought to consult her about it. Or even tell her.

"Princess Ari!" her father nearly shouted, getting her attention.

"I beg your pardon, Sire. I-I was surprised."

"Er, ah, yes, that's understandable, princess. Please pay your respects to your future spouse and his parents."

Ari turned toward King Orolan and his wife, Queen Ruina. She bowed deeply and tried to maintain a pleasant expression on her face, digging her nails into her palms until she knew they bled. She heard her father say three days hence and felt light-headed, then dizzy.

She woke to hear her grandmother say, "I told him to wait until he had a chance to talk to her. No wonder she fainted. At least the prince actually seems to care about her. He nearly knocked his own mother over in his haste to scoop the princess up in his arms, screaming for a physician."

"Well she has no choice but to marry him now, what with him announcing it to the court.

The herald informed the entire city within an hour."

"He should be more worried about the humans so close to the city than me getting married in such a hurry. Why the wild rush?"

"Just how long have you been awake?" her mother demanded before pushing her hair back and feeling her forehead. "Hmph! No fever. Since when do you faint like a simpering maiden still in her first 100 years?"

"Since humans were nearly at our gates trying to kill us, and since father decided I was getting married in three days but didn't think it worth mentioning to me before he told the entire city." Ari sprang from her bed and began pacing, her shock quickly replaced by rage. She clenched her fists and gasped. Looking down, she opened her hands and discovered angry welts where her nails had indeed punctured the skin. Sighing, she spun on her heels and said, "What do I have to do before you kick me out of my home and sell me to these over-eager lechers?"

"Ari!"

"Ari!"

"Sorry, I'm rather annoyed at the moment."

REVENGE OF THE DRAGONS

A handmaiden entered, bowed, and said, "Prince Joran's manservant is here to inquire after Princess Ari's health. He sent these flowers," she added, holding out a large bouquet. "Shall I put them in a vase?"

Ari nodded. "Thank the prince for his kindness and tell him I am feeling much better," Ari said, managing to sound much more calm and polite than she felt. But then she'd been raised to shield her emotions and reactions.

"We're going to leave you alone to actually calm down," her grandmother said.

They no sooner left than her brother appeared. Before she could open her mouth he held up his hands and said, "No, I didn't know a thing. I was as surprised as you. I mean, not that the prince wanted to marry you. He even asked me once if I thought you favored him. I told him to ask you himself. I guess I should have given you a head's up that he was interested in you."

"Don't blame yourself. I already knew he liked me. I could hardly get away from him when they visited. I knew I'd probably have to have an arranged marriage eventually, but I thought father would at least have discussed it with me before just announcing it. I guess I just feel like I've been sold."

"If it makes you feel any better, judging by the gifts that arrived, you have great value."

"I'm sure my dowry wasn't a sow and a cow."

"More likely a mule."

Ari laughed, as her brother intended. He could always make her laugh.

"What will I do without you, Gilivan?"

"You're not moving to the bottom of the ocean."

"I might as well be."

"I've done a bit of investigation on your future husband, Ari. Whatever else he may be, I think you might be interested to know he's a dragon rider."

"What? Are you sure?"

"Positive. And I'll leave you with that interesting fact. It'll give you something to talk to him about at dinner tonight. I'm sure it's shaping up to be a long, drawn-out boring affair. Rest up!"

The three days and a wedding passed quickly. Two weeks on horseback in a caravan of over a hundred warriors, retainers and royalty along with the wagons and weapons needed to sustain and protect them passed slowly.

"We should be home within a few hours, Ari."

"How soon before we'll see dragons overhead?"

Prince Joran laughed and reached over to pat her arm. "I think you're more excited about my dragons than you are meeting your new subjects in Allhluna. That's your home now, Ari."

His tone was gentle, but she detected an underlying steel in his upright posture and rigid shoulders. Tall, long legged, broad chested and muscled. The handsome prince carried himself like a future king, but he already received that kind of respect from those around him. He was a warrior and a leader of warriors and was used to having his orders obeyed without question. He was a dragon rider. She already sensed that obedience would be expected of her too, without him ever lifting a finger.

"Not at all. It's just that we don't have dragons and until lately I didn't know any of the elves still rode them."

He nodded but remained silent.

It was fine with her. She was busy watching the skies. Now that he considered her family, he was happy to answer all her questions. One of the first and most useful things she learned was that their kingdoms had renewed the peace treaty to come to each other's aid nearly as soon as her vows were spoken. This was timely because apparently both the dragon riding humans and nearby orcs had discovered the elven city and intended to attack to gain the treasures rumored to be hidden there.

Ari wondered how long it would be before the humans attacked and what the elves were planning to do about it.

Dinner at the Arahluna Palace was a long and tedious procedure, with strict protocols and hierarchy from the seating to the order of courses. After only a few days Ari was bored to death. The banquets back home had similar pageantry, but at least she knew everyone. She had a long way to go before she knew the court at Arahluna, let alone who among them she could trust. Probably no one.

REVENGE OF THE DRAGONS

To amuse herself, she'd been having a conversation with grandmother. She described what the ladies were wearing, how the men appeared, especially the dragon riders.

Ari was fascinated by Arahluna's dragons. She wanted to ride one and soon. But Joran laughed when she asked to ride one. He reminded her that dragon riders trained and learned the commands and then if they were lucky enough a dragon just might choose them, but there were far more riders than dragons, so it was a rare and coveted honor.

There were female warriors and even a female dragon rider, though Ari had only seen the one. She was surprised to see that there were at least two dozen dragons. Her brother had been surprised when she told him, too.

Perhaps it was the lengthy confinement, the endless waiting for the next royal activity or for Joran to show up and take her for a walk or a ride on horses, never dragons. She watched closely when he rode his dragon. He thought she watched him. He was wrong. Her observation was calculated and intense. She was determined to ride a dragon, no matter what the requirements might be.

Ari began to drink more wine with dinner. It helped alleviate the boredom. Her excitement over the dragons dwindled. She went to bed sooner, slept in later, and lost interest in everything, even talking to grandmother and her brother.

After dinner on the night that marked a week of marital captivity in her new home, Joran came to Ari's bed, kissed her deeply and said, "Tomorrow we leave to join forces with your father's army. The humans and orcs have laid siege to the city. Our dragons will first attack and kill theirs, then wipe out the majority of their forces before the cavalry rides through them to finish them off."

She wanted to ask him something, but he kissed her again, and moved over her. By the time he rose to go to his own chambers because as he told her he would be rising early and wouldn't disturb her, she forgot what she would ask. Before dawn he was gone, according to her servant.

It took another three days for it to occur to her that when she wasn't asleep she was nibbling without hunger but drinking with thirst though she never seemed to get drunk, only tired. Forever tired.

By the fourth day she realized the annoyance she'd been trying to ignore were the telepathic messages of her brother, her mother, her grandmother, her father. She slapped the goblet of water from her servant's hand and stared at the contents as it pooled across the marble floor. Drugged. They were drugging her. But why?

By midafternoon, she was awake. Fully awake. She focused and tried to communicate with first her brother and then her grandmother. She couldn't feel their presence. The messages in her head had stopped. Why? Were they dead? Never in her life had she been unable to reach family. The sudden feel of isolation terrified her.

She went downstairs and saw the queen outside on a bench. Rushing down the steps, she spoke loud enough to be heard over the ocean's surf. "Did the army arrive in time to help my family? Any news of the war?"

As though surprised to see her, the queen said, "They should be returning by tomorrow. All is well."

But all was not well, and Ari knew it, which meant the queen was lying. But why?

The next day she awoke much more clear-headed. She didn't drink any of the wine she was offered and made sure she only drank from a water glass Wren, the servant she brought with her, offered.

Ari paced in her room, angry and afraid. Then seeing no one outside, she used the stairs outside her chamber that led to the sandy beach behind the castle. She followed a long path that led into the caves along the bluff.

Desperate enough to try anything to see how her family was doing and discover why she couldn't hear them, Ari entered the cave. Joran told her a wild dragon no one had managed to tame lived there, and many tried because it was the largest any of them had ever seen.

Her hand shook as she brushed back her hair. She could smell the sulfur and feel the heat from the dragon's breath as soon as she entered the cave. Forcing herself, she moved further into the cave and then stopped. What she thought was a rise in the cave floor wasn't. It was a sleeping dragon that had awakened at her presence.

Too late to go back, she froze. The dragon raised its mammoth head and opened its eyes. Gold and luminous, with slit pupils that looked like a monstrous cat's. It's eyes opened wider and it snorted. Ari managed to keep from shutting her eyes but couldn't resist crouching down and shrinking herself smaller. The dragon's head reached the top of the cave. The creature was massive. Terrifying.

It glared into Ari's eyes, trying to force her to back down, to run in fear.

Ari held her ground and refused to look away.

The dragon shook it's head, then seemed to relax and lowered its right wing, allowing Ari to climb up and into the already attached saddle. Apparently one of the other candidates managed to get it tethered. Clutching the reigns, in ancient Elven she ordered the dragon to fly.

She screamed in terror when the dragon made a sudden movement. He shuffled to the cave's entrance, and then ran a bit before launching itself into the sky. It flew so fast and so high, Ari hung on for her life.

After a bit of experimenting she figured out that the reins worked much the same as those on a horse. Using ancient Elven, she soon had the beast headed home. Her real home.

"Ari, what are you doing? Go back. Now!"

Her husband's voice barked orders into her mind telepathically well enough, though she ignored him and kept heading to reach her family.

She soon saw dragons in flight ahead of her. Only around six remained, cruising above the city, amidst plumes of smoke. She managed to evade them and flew over the city. What she noticed first was that the water had flooded over the dam and into the valley below, nearly draining the lake so that there were no longer any active waterfalls. Next she noticed the stench of burning. The city may have been stone, but stone scorches and the wood beams used for doors and windows burn, as do bodies.

There were elves below her, but all of them wore the uniform of her husband and his armies. She did a flyover but couldn't find a single uniform belonging to her people that wasn't on a corpse either laying where it had fallen or stacked in a pyre of bodies that had already been set ablaze.

"Ari! What are you doing here and how did you get that beast to let you ride it?"

"What happened to my family?"

"That's why I didn't want you to come. We couldn't save them."

Unable to physically shove her husband out of her head she ignored him. She flew over the forest and still couldn't find a single human, orc, or any other enemy to her people. Except her husband and his people. His people. Not her people.

Filled with a blinding rage, she had long since lost the terror she felt upon the huge red dragon beneath her.

She knew what she had to do.

Within an hour there was only one dragon in sight. There were also no live elves within the city. But there was still one blight above her. Ari soared into the sky and her husband urged his dragon to pursue her.

When it became clear that his smaller dragon would outmaneuver her if she continued on the defensive, she changed tactics. She did a turn in motion and flew straight at her husband's dragon and ordered hers to attack the vile, lying murderer before her. Without hesitation, the dragon beneath her charged her husband's dragon and bit it in half, chomping down and eating whatever failed to fall to the charred earth below.

The woods were ablaze, the strong wind carrying the fires to the north. Tears streamed down Ari's face as she landed within the city to look for survivors. Her excitement over dragons was gone forever. No one wins when dragons are used for revenge, she thought.

She probably would never know why the prince wanted to marry her and keep her safe from the flames, but there was no going back, and nothing left of her home to salvage. She would have to fly north until she found somewhere safe to start over.

***